KT-443-924

THE LAST OF THE SPIRITS

Also by Chris Priestley

The Dead Men Stood Together
The Dead of Winter
Through Dead Eyes

*

The Tales of Terror Collection:
Uncle Montague's Tales of Terror
Tales of Terror from the Black Ship
Tales of Terror from the Tunnel's Mouth
Christmas Tales of Terror

hire County Council

DISCARDED

014012883 X

THE LAST OF THE SPIRITS

CHRIS PRIESTLEY

BLOOMSBURY

LONDON   NEW DELHI   NEW YORK   SYDNEY

Bloomsbury Publishing, London, New Delhi, New York and Sydney

First published in Great Britain in November 2014 by Bloomsbury Publishing Plc
50 Bedford Square, London WC1B 3DP

www.bloomsbury.com
www.chrispriestleybooks.com

Bloomsbury is a registered trademark of Bloomsbury Publishing Plc

Copyright © Chris Priestley 2014

The moral rights of the author have been asserted

All rights reserved
No part of this publication may be reproduced or
transmitted by any means, electronic, mechanical, photocopying
or otherwise, without the prior permission of the publisher

A CIP catalogue record for this book is available from the British Library

ISBN 978 1 4088 5413 6

Typeset by Hewer Text UK Ltd, Edinburgh
Printed and bound in Great Britain by CPI Group (UK) Ltd, Croydon CR0 4YY

1 3 5 7 9 10 8 6 4 2

For Philippa

Chapter 1

The boy had never spoken to the old man before, nor scarcely noticed him. The old man, had he been asked, would have sworn under oath, hand on the Bible, that he had likewise never seen the boy.

But the truth was, over the last few years, they had passed within inches of each other a hundred times. The old man had even brushed the boy aside more than once as he beetled his way to his office.

To the old man, the boy was just another tiresome obstacle to be avoided. To the boy, the old man, along with all the other hard-faced strangers like him, was yet another reason to hate the world.

But this day, this chill and fog-choked Christmas Eve – this day was to be different.

'Mister,' cried the boy, wiping his nose on the back of his hand.

The old man flinched but did not turn, his black-coated back bent over as though heading into a strong wind, the silver tip of his cane tick-tick-ticking on the paving slabs as he hurried along. *Tick-tick-tick*. Time is money. The boy sped up and pulled his sister along in his wake.

'Mister!'

This time the boy emphasised his cry with a tug on the old man's coat-tail. This had an immediate effect. The old man skidded in his tracks and turned round with a ferocious look on his face, a look that might have made another faint. The children were well used to such expressions. They stopped, but kept their distance.

'What do you want?' hissed the old man, his muffler pulled up to his bottom lip, his hat jammed down on to his furrowed brow so that his white eyebrows curled round the black brim. His eyes were ice blue.

'Please, sir,' said the boy. 'We wondered, as it's Christmas Eve and all, if you might see your way to giving us a few coins, sir. Only we –'

'Oh, you did, did you?' said the man, narrowing his eyes still further, their reddened rims the only warm colour in his deathly face. 'You thought as it was Christmas Eve and the season of goodwill, you'd rob me, did you?'

'We ain't robbing no one,' said the boy. 'We're asking is all. A few coins. That ain't a crime, is it?'

The old man raised his cane and bared his crooked yellow teeth.

'Get away from me or I'll call a constable!' he cried. 'Maybe I'll give you a thrashing before he arrives.'

The boy and girl ran, clattering round a corner into an alleyway, where the boy grabbed his sister and turned to peer at the old man, a vague smudge now in

3

the fog as he climbed the three stone stairs to his office, opened the black door and slammed it behind him.

The violence of that slam seemed to shake the street and it dislodged a great icicle from the roof, which dropped like an arrow to shatter on the pavement below. The snow of the week before had thawed from most of the roofs on the street, but clearly the old man's office was a few degrees colder than the houses on either side. In any event, what had thawed was now speedily refreezing.

The slamming door seemed likewise to dislodge something in the boy's mind. It was not the old man's refusal to give them money, nor his threat to call a constable – both were common enough occurrences; no, it was the look in the old man's eye, that look of cold contempt. It had pierced the boy to the bone. He walked back and stood in a patch of waste ground opposite the old man's office, staring malevolently.

'Sam,' said his sister, walking up behind him, 'let's go. I'm cold.'

'Go where?' he hissed, without taking his eyes from the shining black door. 'What does it matter where we go, Lizzie? We'll be as cold there as here.'

She tugged at his arm, and he shrugged her away.

'No one's making you stay,' he said. 'Go if you want to.'

Lizzie turned and began to walk, slipping and sliding on the ice and slush. Her boots were so ragged and over-sized it would have been a comic sight were her arms not so very thin, her face so pale and gaunt, and her eyes so sunken and terribly lacking in any of life's sparkle.

'Wait!' said Sam with an angry sigh and ran to catch up with her.

At thirteen, he was older by three years but not much taller and not much heavier either. His face was just as gaunt as his sister's, but there was a hard-ness in his features that was absent in hers. His brow was furrowed by a constant frown and his jaw thrust out, daring the world to hit him. His hands were locked in fists, even when he slept.

They worked the streets, stretching out their filthy hands to anyone who passed, dipping them lightly into pockets and purses if they got the chance.

Christmas Eve was a time when most folk had some extra warmth in their hearts, but this warmth was directed towards their loved ones in the main. So very little was left over for those who needed it most.

By mid-afternoon Sam and Lizzie had made only enough to buy a very small pie between them. And by that time most people were already heading home, let out early on account of the coming festivities. Tired and still hungry, the two children found themselves back on that same piece of inhospitable waste ground opposite the old man's office.

A handsome young man walked down the street, whistling. He skipped up the steps to the door and rapped on the knocker, blowing into his hands. The door opened and he walked in. As the door was closing, Sam set off across the road.

'Sam?' said Lizzie.

'Come on,' he said, without turning round.

'What are we doing?'

Sam didn't answer. He didn't know the answer. He just felt drawn in somehow. He walked up to the railings in front of the window. Through the dusty glass he could see the old man's bony back as he worked at a desk. Sam strained his ears to hear.

'A merry Christmas, Uncle,' came a cry from inside as the young man walked through from the hall.

'Bah!' muttered the old man. 'Humbug!'

Sam ducked behind the railings as the young man came into view. It was clearly no warmer inside the office than outside, for Sam could see his breath.

There followed some muffled conversation. Sam was unable to make out many of the words until the old man shouted, making Lizzie jump.

'Nephew!' he yelled. 'Keep Christmas in your own way and let me keep it in mine.'

So the old man was this fellow's uncle. Sam had not imagined him to have any family. He clearly did not want any, even so. Every attempt at goodwill from the nephew was met with the same sourness the old man had shown to them.

A clerk was standing nearby and at one point forgot himself and applauded the nephew's words. His expression made it all too clear that he realised his mistake as he became suddenly interested in attending to the fire.

'Let me hear another sound from *you*,' cried his employer harshly, 'and you'll keep your Christmas by losing your situation.'

'Poor man,' whispered Lizzie, seeing the clerk's pale face.

'Don't be angry, Uncle,' said the nephew, stepping between the old man and his clerk. 'Come! Dine with us tomorrow.'

But the old man would have none of it. The more the nephew persisted, the ruder he became. The nephew's jolly parting cry of 'Merry Christmas' was greeted with an emphatically snarled 'Good afternoon!' as was the

'Happy New Year!' that followed it. Eventually even this good-natured young man was forced to admit defeat and headed towards the outer door.

As it opened, Sam and Lizzie could hear the nephew wishing the clerk a merry Christmas and getting a far warmer response. Through the window glass, they caught the old man muttering. It was as though goodwill caused him pain.

At that very moment two men arrived at the door, well turned out – heavy coats, top hats on their heads. The nephew stepped to one side with a hearty 'Good day, gentlemen!'

He was as cheerful as the old man was dour and, after wishing them too a merry Christmas, he strode away up the street as though, for him, Christmas could not start a minute too soon. The two men were duly let in and the door closed behind them.

'Come on, Liz,' said Sam.

He had seen enough, and they walked away. The visitors had not been inside the office for more than a few minutes, however, when they emerged, looking as though they had been hauled before a hanging judge and had only just escaped the gallows. They crossed the street towards Sam and Lizzie, their faces pale and shocked.

'Well!' said one to the other as they stood nearby. 'Have you ever heard the like?'

'Never put so forcibly,' said his companion, opening a box of snuff and taking a pinch. 'Many do not want to give to charity, but few are so *proud* of it.'

He sniffed loudly, sucking the snuff up inside his flared nostrils.

'*Are there no prisons?*' said the first, mimicking the old man's voice.

'*And the Union Poorhouses,*' said the other, doing the same, hunching his shoulders and twisting his face into a sour expression, a few rogue strands of snuff still visible. '*Are they still in operation?*'

'And when you said that many would not go there and would rather die –'

'*Then they had better do it*,' said the other in the old man's voice, '*and decrease the surplus population.*'

The two men stood and looked back at the office in wonder.

'It is a shame that Mr Marley is deceased,' said the first. 'For he must surely have been a kinder soul than Mr Scrooge.'

Scrooge. It was a name that prodded like a bony finger. *Scrooge*. Sam's eyes narrowed as he stared resentfully at the black door and the black heart it guarded. The two charity men had walked away before he realised he should have asked them for money. Soft heads or soft hearts, those types were always good for a tap.

So old Scrooge thought that the poor should die rather than trouble him? This was hardly a novel view in London town and Sam might have found a dozen men nearby who felt the same. But few – very few – would say the words out loud.

The light of day had faded already and Sam

winced at the thought of the pain the night's chill would bring. How many more nights could he endure? he wondered. How many more would Lizzie survive? The empty suits in the window of the tailor's across the way were warmer than they were. Why, a plucked goose in the butcher shop had more love and care lavished on it than was ever gifted to them.

Sam was filled with a bitter, seething, murderous rage against all who lived in comfort and security in that cold-hearted city, and this fury was funnelled and concentrated down, like a hammer to a nail, on to the head of Mr Scrooge.

'Sam,' said Lizzie, seeing his fierce trance, 'I'm cold.'

'We're all cold,' said Sam mechanically.

'Please, Sam,' she said quietly.

Sam turned away from his vigil.

'Look,' he said after a moment, his eyes lifeless, like glass marbles. 'There's a fire.'

Ahead of them a small group huddled round a brazier lit by workmen, heads bowed like mourners at a funeral pyre. The happy yellow glow seemed alien to that colourless place and it attracted the cold and homeless as animals to a desert oasis.

The two children shoved through those already gathered. No one gave way for them. There was no more sympathy to be had there than from the old man who had shunned them. The smaller you were, the closer to the ground and closer to the grave pit, that was all.

They were not the only children there for one thing. A woman, whose features shifted and blurred in the heat of the flames, held a baby to her breast under her filthy shawl, its tiny head just peeping out. The mother stared blankly into the fire, so weak she looked as though she might fall headlong into it. Would she see Christmas Day? Would the child?

The fire was a feeble one, and Sam looked about for anything that would burn. Builders clearing a house nearby had thrown things down into the yard below. Sam rummaged around and came back hugging pieces of wood and several books to his chest.

As he was about to throw one of the books on the fire, it opened and the pages fluttered, revealing for a fleeting second a brightly coloured illustration, partly hidden under a sheet of tissue paper. It was like an exotic butterfly.

'Don't,' said Lizzie, grabbing his arm.

'What? You'd rather keep it, would you? You'd rather carry it around, would you, so's you can read it to yourself when you're tucked up in bed, eh?'

A one-eyed man nearby sniggered wheezily.

'No,' said Lizzie. 'But –'

'But what?' said Sam, more loudly now, and more cruelly. 'What?'

'It's just too lovely to burn,' she said, not quite swallowing a sob.

Sam shook his head. Too lovely to burn! The one-eyed man shook his head too, and Sam was momentarily troubled by this distorted mirror of himself.

'We could sell it,' protested Lizzie.

'Half the pages is missing,' said Sam. 'No one's going to want to buy that.'

'But –'

'You're too sentimental, Liz. That's your trouble.'

Sam tossed the book on to the fire and it fell, pages open, the flames eating up the words. Lizzie was able to catch the odd phrase before the fire blackened the paper and tore it up, sending glowing fragments high into the night.

Sam saw the words too, but understood nothing. Writing was a mystery to him: a cryptic code without a key. Books! What better use for them than fuel for a fire? He'd have burned every book in London even if it only kept his hands warm for a moment. What were stories but just another kind of lie?

Sam turned away from the brazier. He could still see the office dimly through the fog and the dark. As he watched, the door opened and a man stood briefly silhouetted in the light from inside before hunching himself against the cold and striding away down the street on stick-thin legs.

This wasn't the old man's hunched gait, but the brisker step of someone younger. It was the clerk to old Scrooge, a man as thin as Sam with clothes that had seen better days, though the clerk might struggle to bring them to mind. Not long before, Scrooge had threatened to sack him, but outside the office the clerk was like a bird released from a cage.

He whistled gaily and would have no doubt flown if tattered coat-tails had been wings. He went on his way, chuckling to himself as he took a run and slid along the pavement for a yard or two, almost falling over.

Two plump children on their way home with their mother laughed at the clerk's antics, but their gentle mockery only lightened his mood further. He tipped his hat to them and bowed elaborately before he hopped and skipped nimbly across the road to walk within a few feet of Sam.

'Merry Christmas!' he said, throwing his scarf over his shoulder and blowing into his thin pale fingers.

'Merry Christmas!' said Lizzie with a smile.

The clerk rubbed his hands together and walked on, whistling again.

'What have you got to be merry-Christmas-ing about?' hissed Sam with a snarl. 'Merry Christmas? Pah! It's all right for him.'

Lizzie began to sob. There was a time – although it already seemed another life ago – when this would have melted the iciest of Sam's moods, but his heart was as hard as iron now. He simply looked away towards the old man, hidden behind that inky door.

And then, like ink, the night's true darkness came flowing in and with it a bone-gnawing cold. The crowd about the fire was growing, but they needed to find shelter. Some nights had killer written on them and this, thought Sam, was one of them. Only the fit and healthy would survive the deadly creeping frost that would be coming soon – and who on the street was fit or healthy?

Sam peered at the door of Scrooge's office and his heart blackened to match it. The fog seemed to blur all the rest of London town and leave only that black rectangle in focus. Then all at once it opened and out stepped old Scrooge, looking about as cautiously as a fox and locking the door behind him.

The old man set off along the pavement, his cane tick-ticking as before, his head tucked into his hunched shoulders that were themselves pulled into his bony, crooked back. There was no festive lightness in his step, no 'Merry Christmas' from him as he passed others on the street. No greeting was offered and none returned.

'Come on, Lizzie,' said Sam, walking after the old man.

Lizzie didn't even ask where they were going. She trusted Sam and knew she would not be alive without his wits. He always managed to find some scrap of food, some kind of shelter. He had saved her life a hundred times.

Sam saw the beetle-black shape of the old man ahead in the failing light and fog and hurried to make sure they did not lose him. *Tick-tick-tick.* The cane and its echo rattled ahead of them like loose teeth.

Eventually they came to a dimly lit and dreary yard. The old man looked about him but did not see them. He walked into the yard and Sam and Lizzie waited at the entrance as he fumbled in his pocket for a bunch of keys. So this was where he lived. This was his den.

Sam looked on. As soon as the old man opened the door, he would attack him. He had a length of lead piping in his coat pocket that he had picked up when he had fetched the books for the fire. He would knock Scrooge down and they would rob him. He would not set out to kill him, but some men's skulls were thinner than others.

Sam was puzzled to hear the old man talking. At

first he thought there was someone else there, but he soon realised that Scrooge was talking to himself, muttering wildly and shaking his head like he was fresh out of Bedlam. He seemed for all the world to be talking to his own door knocker!

Somehow this eccentric behaviour blackened Sam's mood still further. It outraged him. It goaded him. Why should a witless old fool like this live in comfort and plenty whilst they starved and froze?

A crisp, wintery contempt for the old man settled on Sam's heart like a rime of frost that all the heat of the Indies could not have melted. It felt good. All these years of hating the world had made him feel powerless, but now he had but one target. He would make this one man pay and that would be enough.

Yet for all the mounting violence of his thoughts, Sam did not launch his attack. He felt a sudden unfamiliar heaviness in his legs. The old man had gone inside and closed the door behind him before Sam was able to cross the yard. He walked towards the door and looked at the knocker hanging there. It was an ugly thing to be sure, with a strange face, its features caught somewhere betwixt man and lion, a dull brass ring clamped between its teeth. Sam stood there staring so long that Lizzie tugged the sleeve of his jacket.

'Sam?' she said. 'Sam?'

He snapped out of his trance at the sound of Lizzie's weak and plaintive voice. He looked around and pointed to a tall, old, arched iron gate on the other side of the cobbled yard.

'Come on, Liz,' he said. 'Over here.'

The gate opened with a reluctant, guttural groan that seemed disconcertingly human, and they squeezed through to find themselves in a walled churchyard, soot-blackened headstones all about them etched with skulls and hourglasses and other such reminders of mortality. Black and leafless trees stood here and there like clutching hands. Sam walked up to the chapel door, but it was locked and with a lock that was not going to be shifted or broken.

'Here,' said Sam, walking back to Lizzie. 'This'll have to do.'

He was pointing at a tomb that had once stood like a great stone bed, etched all over with moss-filled letters telling the story of the man whose body lay forgotten by all but the worms. It was now in a state of partial collapse, one side having fallen away to make a little web-strewn cave beneath the huge slab.

The quiet churchyard was sheltered by walls and the church itself, and the tombstone cave added a little more. It was a grim place to spend the night, but they had slept in worse. They squeezed together for warmth as the fog thickened around them.

Sam marvelled at how easily Lizzie could fall asleep, no matter the circumstances. He felt the length of lead piping he had picked up on the waste ground by Scrooge's office. It felt colder and even heavier now. He clung to it as a small child might cling to a favourite doll.

Chapter 2

Sam woke with a start, bumping his head on the stone slab above him. He took a few seconds to remember where he was, but he could see nothing in the gloom that shouldn't have been there. Lizzie was still breathing gently beside him. All seemed as well as could be, so he settled back down to sleep.

But no sooner had he closed his eyes than a low moan emanated from somewhere nearby. Yes – that was the noise that had woken him, he realised. Was it the gate? he wondered. Was a constable or church warden coming to turf them out? On Christmas Eve? Unlikely. They would all be snugly at home with their loved ones.

The moan sounded again, more loudly this time, and Sam knew straight away it was not the old hinges of any gate. For one thing, it was coming from *under* the ground. He could *feel* it, as well as hear it.

Sam shifted his position and peered out from their hideaway. On the opposite side of the snow-covered pathway was a plain, arched headstone. The stone bore the name and dates of the man whose bones lay beneath, but Sam could not read them.

The groan came again and the little linked chain that marked the boundary of that grave now rattled, sending showers of sparkling frost to the ground.

Sam tried to make sense of it. His thoughts seemed to blunder about his head like men in a dark room. A shaking of the ground – what did they call it? . . . A quake . . . an earthquake! Is that what this was? An earthquake?

But even as he wondered if the buildings all about would come crashing down around them, with old Scrooge and his money buried under his own house, and Sam and Lizzie buried under the rubble of the church, something started to emerge from the ground in front of the headstone.

Sam stared wide-eyed with incredulity as the mysterious translucent dome became, by slow degrees, the forehead, eyebrows, eyes, nose, mouth and chin of a long and cheerless face, all bound together by a scarf wrapped under the chin and tied in a bow atop a balding head.

The head was not alone. Shoulders soon appeared, clothed in a worn black topcoat, and then a matching chest with dull buttons down the front and a waist-coat and watch chain, and britches and boots and, lo and behold, a whole man now stood there.

Not a *whole* man in truth – for much of what he was and had been still lay beneath the earth he had been planted in. Sam could glimpse the headstone through the man's legs – and not due to his standing with his legs apart, but on account of his legs and his britches being not quite as solid as they might be, so that for Sam it was like looking through a picture of a saint on a stained-glass window.

Those saints of old often carry something with them in those pictures – the instrument of their martyrdom in many cases – and this figure, noticed Sam, carried something of that kind too. He held a great length of rusting iron chains, the like of which a murderous convict would be forced to wear, but with links so grim and mighty they could just as readily have been used to moor a convict *ship* as to restrain the felons who were caged aboard her.

The ghost – for Sam could reach no other conclusion, try as he might, that this was indeed a phantom of some sort – gave another terrible, low, gurgling groan and shivered, jangling his massive chains, and every one of Sam's nerves to boot. Sam lost his grip on the stone to which he had been clinging and tumbled out on to the path at the spectre's feet.

He glanced at Lizzie, who slept on oblivious, and then up at the fearful apparition looming above him.

The apparition, for his part, slowly looked down, cocking his head and raising a ghostly eyebrow as though regarding a particularly malformed breed of pigeon.

Then all at once he puffed out his translucent chest and lurched forward, the sole of his boot falling towards Sam's face like a black sack.

Sam cried out, but the boot passed through him without harm, although not without some sensation. It did not cause him pain, but he felt a damp, chill wind blowing through his head and with it an awful, aching sadness and longing of a degree and keenness he had rarely felt, however low his fortunes had fallen.

The ghost walked on, dragging the chains behind him like the train of a bridal robe. They too passed through Sam's prone body with a similar sensation, but with added sound, as the links scraped and rattled one against the other. It was a noise so jarring and unsettling that Sam did not think he could bear it another second, and he instinctively reached out to grab them.

To his great surprise, despite their insubstantial appearance, his hands gained enough purchase on the chains to grab hold, and as the ghost took his next step, the chain tightened and brought him to a halt.

The spectre stood there a moment, his back to Sam, his head bowed a little, his whole body framed within the arched gateway through which Sam and Lizzie had entered. Then he turned slowly and walked back. Sam dropped the chains and tried to get up, but the chains still lay across his legs and seemed to weigh him down.

The ghost stopped in front of him, reached up to the top of his head with both hands and untied the knot in the scarf. Before Sam could say a word, the scarf came loose, and with it the ghost's lower jaw. The chin now dropped to his chest, his huge mouth lolling open like the entrance to hell itself.

'No . . . no . . . please,' muttered Sam, putting his hands over his face. 'I can't . . . This can't . . . I must be dreaming.'

'Who are you?' said the ghost, his voice seeming to arrive on that same sad and chill wind that had passed through Sam a moment before. It came from the ghost's mouth, but it also came from everywhere. And nowhere. It swirled around the churchyard, pursued by its own feeble echo.

'Sam,' he replied. 'Sir.'

'And what business do you have with me?' said the ghost.

The words chased each other through the headstones.

'I don't,' said Sam. 'I just . . . I don't even know what – who – you are.'

'I was that man once.' The ghost pointed to the headstone by the grave from which he had risen. 'Do you see my marker? Do you see the name writ there upon it?'

Sam looked and nodded. The ghost raised a sceptical eyebrow.

'You cannot read?'

Sam shook his head. The ghost frowned.

'Jacob Marley was my name in life, boy. I was much taken with it when I lived. I no longer know the reason why. Such vanities are a forgotten thing to me now.'

Marley? Sam was sure he had heard the name before but could not for the moment place it.

'That filthy headstone, unloved by all but frost and moss, is all there is to show I ever walked these streets. I left no children to mourn my passing.'

The ghost shook his head wearily and muttered something Sam did not catch.

'But I must away,' he resumed. 'Time moves on and I have a soul to save. Or at least I have a part to play in its salvation. Or possible salvation, at any rate . . .'

The voice trailed away.

'How about lifting these chains off me before you

go?' said Sam. 'I don't like to bother you, but them things make a dreadful din, you know. Goes right through you.'

Marley's ghost nodded and stooped over, lifting up a length of the chains and letting Sam scrabble free. Then he threw the chains over one shoulder like a cloak.

'What's the story with the chains anyway?' said Sam, feeling a little emboldened now he was free. 'Are you on a leash?'

Again the unearthly voice surged up from the black cave of the spectre's mouth.

'No,' said Marley's ghost. 'The chains are not to bind me. They are to *remind* me.'

The word 'remind' echoed around the graveyard, bouncing from tombstone to tombstone.

'Remind you of what?' said Sam. 'Are you – *were* you – a blacksmith or something? Or maybe you were buried under a load of chains. Is that how you, er, you know . . . ?'

Marley's ghost closed his eyes for a moment and seemed lost in memories.

'No,' he replied. 'I did not die in a shipyard accident. Nor did I spend my days at the forge. I was nothing so skilled nor so useful. I was a money man. I worked not far from here in a counting house. We lent money to those who needed it and charged them steeply for the privilege. You know the sort of man?'

Sam nodded grimly. He had seen their work. Half the people on the streets were there with a little help from money men. Sam and Lizzie were among their number.

'These are the chains I forged for my soul in life and these are the chains I am bound to wear in death. Every link on them I made myself – not by a blacksmith's skill and honest labour, but rather through my own greed and selfishness. I had not even the wit to be happy at another man's expense; I simply sought to be richer, as though that, of itself, were some kind of achievement. Never was there a more pointless existence.'

Sam's own existence felt far more pointless but he decided not to debate the point. The ghost seemed to read his mind.

'But do not think these chains are bought with gold lust, boy,' he said. 'These links are not forged in heat, but by cold hearts. Money-making gives you the means to be heartless, but it doesn't give you a monopoly on heartlessness. You have a chain yourself if you could but see it.'

'What?' said Sam, looking down at his feet.

'Yes,' said Marley's ghost, peering at Sam and nodding. 'And while it's not as long as mine, it's longer than it ought to be for one so young.'

'Well, that ain't fair!' said Sam.

Marley's ghost shrugged and took out his pocket watch.

'I have no time to parley with the likes of you, lad,' he said, turning away and heading for the gateway once again. 'This is my purpose and I must do as I am bid. Three spirits will follow me. The first will show the past, the second of them the present and the third will reveal the future. They shall show this man the error of his ways.'

'Yeah?' said Sam, still trying to see the invisible chain he was supposed to have about him. 'Who's that then?'

'My old partner in the firm,' said the ghost, passing through the bars of the gate without opening it. 'Ebenezer Scrooge.'

Sam jumped to his feet as the ends of Marley's chains rattled by like metal pythons. Marley was already halfway across the yard, his feet sinking into the ground at each step. By the time Sam reached the churchyard gates, Marley was only visible from the chest up and he moved forward as though wading out to sea.

'You mean to say you're going to help that old miser?' yelled Sam. 'You're here to save that sinner?

Why does he get a second chance? Let him rot in hell if that's what he's good for. Let him get crushed under a mountain of chains. It ain't fair!'

But Marley's ghost walked on without regard for the fairness of the situation and heedless of Sam's outraged cries. Now there was just the top of Marley's head, the scarf retied; now there was nothing.

'It – ain't – fair!' yelled Sam.

'What ain't?' said a voice behind him. Sam turned to see Lizzie rubbing her eyes and squinting at him suspiciously. 'Who are you yelling at?'

'Everyone,' he muttered darkly. 'Every-stinking-one.'

Chapter 3

When Lizzie had asked Sam why they were leaving the relative comfort and security of the churchyard in the middle of the night, he said that the temperature was dropping and they needed to find somewhere out of the worst of the freezing fog.

This was not all lie – the cold was biting hard. It had become colder by several degrees when Marley had appeared from his grave. For her part Lizzie did not argue. Sam always knew best. And she was so very, very cold.

'But there's a light on,' said Lizzie as they approached Scrooge's house, assuming they would spend the night in an outhouse as they had done so many times before. But they had always waited for the house to go dark. A light might mean a dog or a servant, or both.

'Never mind about that,' said Sam, without turning round.

Sam felt for the comforting weight of the length of lead piping in his coat pocket. The door to the alleyway alongside the house was bolted but it took him only seconds to climb over and open it from the other side.

The alleyway was dark and smelled of cats and damp and blocked drains. The back door was locked with something more substantial than a bolt and the downstairs windows were protected with wrought iron bars.

None of this deterred Sam; on the contrary, security like this meant that there must have been something worth stealing in the house. A lock was an advert. It was a handwritten invitation in copper-plate script. He looked up and grinned like a wolf. Of course the old miser had not gone to the expense of barring the upstairs windows. Sam would make him pay heavily for that piece of penny-pinching.

There was a bend in a drainpipe low enough for him to climb up on, and he helped Lizzie to follow. Ironically, the iron cage over the downstairs window allowed another firm foothold. From there it was an easy climb up the side of the house to the top of the wall that housed the alleyway door.

'I don't like it,' said Lizzie with a whimper. 'It's too high . . .'

'*Shhh*, Lizzie,' hissed Sam. 'Don't look down and you'll be fine, honest. I'm just going to edge over there and get the window open. Hang on.'

Lizzie was not at all convinced.

'Supposing there's someone there, Sam.'

'Stop worrying, Liz.'

He left her standing on the wall, clinging nervously to another drainpipe, and stepped on to where the pipe branched sideways to grab hold of the crumbling sill of the upstairs window. The drainpipe

sagged under his weight and a shower of mortar fell
to the yard below.

Sam tested the pipe and, feeling sure that it was
going to hold firm, edged further up the slope of it,
so that he could more easily raise himself up to see
over the sill.

The stone was cold to the touch and the lead piping
in his pocket clanged against the brickwork as he
peered slowly over the top at the grimy window above.

The glass was so filthy, in fact, the image it grudg-
ingly revealed was blurred and it took a moment for
Sam to realise that Marley's ghost was walking backwards, heading for the window, Scrooge ghostly
visible through the spectre's black topcoat, like something pickled in a jar.

Sam cursed and ducked down, clambering back to
Lizzie, who was about to ask what the matter was
when the sash window above them lurched open.
Sam clamped his hands over her mouth to stop the
scream he was sure was going to come if she caught

sight of Scrooge, let alone Marley's ghost. But to his surprise, Lizzie was not looking at the open window. She was staring up at the sky. He glanced back at the window and saw Scrooge doing the same.

Sam almost cried out himself when he followed their gaze. The murky sky above their heads was swarming with spirits – ghosts like Marley – who swam through the foggy clouds like herring through silted waters. He took his hand away from Lizzie's mouth but she did not scream. They both stared in silent, wide-eyed wonder.

'What . . . are . . . they?' whispered Lizzie eventually.

'Ghosts,' whispered Sam.

'But you always said there was no such thing,' replied Lizzie.

'Yeah. It turns out I was wrong about that.'

The spirits flew and wailed as they went, their mouths mournfully open, their dark eyes yearning, each face a mask of tragedy as sad as any grave-yard angel.

In a doorway on the opposite side of the street, a mother had settled down, a small child huddled under her shawl. She looked exhausted and hung her head, oblivious to the ghost who hovered twenty feet above her head, a great metal safe hanging from his ankle by a chain.

The ghost looked down at her with a look of desperate sorrow etched on to his face. He seemed to struggle to maintain his position, as if against a wind. He moaned and wrung his hands. He reached out as though to help her, but then moaned pitifully again before floating away like a silk scarf on a sudden breeze.

Then suddenly Marley himself shot by, bursting out of Scrooge's window and joining the flock of ghosts circling in the mist above them. The moaning was deafening and Sam put his hands to his ears. But it did no good.

'What?' said Lizzie, looking at Sam's grimacing face.

'That noise,' yelled Sam. 'How can you stand it?'

'I can't hear nothing,' said Lizzie, confused.

'What? You must do. All them ghosts are crying out. How can you not?'

'I just see their mouths moving,' whispered Lizzie. 'I can't hear nothing.'

'Are you deaf?' Sam shouted, exasperated.

'I can hear you well enough!' she said, frowning.

Sam looked up at Scrooge's window. The old man had closed it after Marley's ghost but Sam wondered if he had been composed enough to remember the latch. He hoped not. It would just be a matter of levering it open. He had to get out of this cacophony. It seemed to be inside him now, rattling his very bones.

Sam climbed up again and peered in. He was right: Scrooge hadn't put the latch on properly. He hadn't even closed the curtains on the window, although he had closed all the curtains round his bed so that he was hidden from view. More to the point, as far as Sam was concerned, the old man could not see them either. All they had to do was wait until he was asleep. He climbed back down to Lizzie.

'Not long now, Liz,' he said.

'What are we waiting for?' she asked, moving her head round and round as she followed a flying spirit above her. 'You said there was no one there. I don't like it here, Sam.'

'You want to go back to that churchyard, do you?' said Sam angrily. 'Where do you think all these ghosts are coming from?'

'No . . . but . . .'

'Well, then,' said Sam.

The clock on a nearby church began to chime. One . . . two . . . three . . . four . . . five . . . six . . . seven . . . eight . . . nine . . . ten . . . eleven . . . twelve.

'Twelve?' said Sam. 'That can't be right. It was midnight when we was in that churchyard. I heard the same clock chime the same hour. What the hell's going on, Liz?'

Lizzie was startled by the question. Sam had never ever asked her opinion about anything before. Never. Not once. It couldn't be a good thing that he was asking now.

There was a sudden burst of light from Scrooge's bedroom. It was the brightest thing they had ever seen, as though a bomb had noiselessly exploded. It lit up the whole street for an instant, throwing shadows across the fog.

'What was that?' said Sam, climbing back up to peer through the window.

When he looked in he saw that the old man's bed curtains were open. The bed itself was now empty. The door was still closed and little points of light lit up the gloom like fireflies, before they were snuffed out one by one.

The first of the spirits had arrived as Marley's ghost had said it would. It must have taken him away somehow. Spirits could probably do anything they liked, thought Sam. He climbed back down to fetch Lizzie.

'Come on,' he said. 'There's no one there, I promise.'

'I can't,' said Lizzie. 'I'm too scared.'

'Don't be daft,' said Sam.

'It's too far. It's too high. I'll fall.'

'You won't fall, Liz. All you have to do is –' Sam's face became suddenly very still and serious.

'Lizzie,' he said slowly. 'Don't turn round.'

Naturally, Lizzie turned round.

Sam clamped his hand over Lizzie's mouth again, but some of her scream still managed to squeeze through his filthy fingers to mingle with the unholy din of the ghostly choir around them. Floating just a few feet away, level with them but hovering above the alleyway they had walked through, was the ghost of a woman, her pale and terrible face contorted by sadness, her hands reaching out towards Lizzie.

The ghost's white throat showed a blue lesion, the mark of a rope clearly visible round her neck. Was she hanged, Sam wondered, or had she been driven by misfortune to take her own life? Her face was a portrait of hopelessness, framed in black despair.

Lizzie almost shoved Sam from the wall in her urgency to access the drainpipe, and no rat could have scaled it quicker. She was over the sill and in through the window before Sam could blink an eye, and he needed no further persuasion to join her as the ghost threw back her head and let out a terrible, despairing moan.

Sam slammed the window shut behind him. Lizzie was sitting on the rug nearby, sobbing to herself.

'Come on,' he said. 'You're inside now.'

'Those ghosts . . .'

'They ain't going to bother you in here.'

Lizzie wiped her nose with her sleeve.

'It ain't that,' she said with another sob. 'They looked so sad, Sam.'

'What do you mean?' he asked. Although he knew exactly what she meant.

'Their faces,' she replied, tears dripping down her cheeks. 'It was horrible, Sam. Horrible.'

Sam shook his head and sighed.

'Only you could feel sorry for a load of bleeding ghosts, Liz,' he said. 'What's it to you if they're sad? Maybe they deserve to be sad, eh? Maybe they was horrible people when they was alive.'

She sniffed and rubbed her eyes.

'But I think that's why they're sad. I think they want to help people now and they can't. Like the ghost what was looking at the woman on the doorstep across the road. I think he wanted to help her but he couldn't. And that's why they're sad. Cos they could have helped when they was alive. And now they can't.'

This was the longest speech Sam thought he had ever heard Lizzie give in the entirety of her short life. Why did she care? Why did she still care? It was a mystery to him as inscrutable as the heavens or the fathomless deeps of the sea.

'Look, there's a fire,' he said after a while. 'It ain't much but it's something. Go and warm yourself.'

Lizzie settled herself down, holding her hands over the meagre embers. The pathetic fire seemed to throb, its red glow fluttering and faintly pulsating like a weak heart. Lizzie felt in need of comfort and asked a question she had asked many times before.

'Tell me about the house by the river, Sam.'

'No.'

This was a response she had heard almost as many times.

'Please . . .'

'No,' said Sam, more fiercely.

Lizzie scowled into the hearth. The chimney made a low whimpering noise.

'Just get warm, Liz.'

'What about you? What are you going to do?'

'Me?' Sam said, pulling the bedding from Scrooge's bed and lifting the mattress. 'I'm going on a treasure hunt.'

Chapter 4

Sam set off on a search of every grimy inch of Scrooge's bedroom, even prising up a loose floor-board and standing on a chest to look at the filthy canopy above the old man's bed, but he found nothing at all save for dust and cockroaches.

He sat back, muttering a low, angry incantation of curses. It infuriated him all the more that this man was rich and chose to live in squalor. It was another kind of selfishness. What was the point of having all that money if he wasn't going to spend it? It was a waste. He didn't deserve to have it.

But more to the point, where was it? Where was all the money? It must be somewhere. A man like

Scrooge would never trust it to a bank. He wouldn't trust anyone. Sam wondered if it was all locked away in a safe at Scrooge's office. But no – he'd want it close. Sam would want it close if it was him.

And what about the old miser? Perhaps Sam ought to wait until he came back and make the old man tell him where the money was. He smiled to himself at the thought. Put the fear of God into the old devil and see what happened. If he didn't tell . . . Well – he'd only have himself to blame for what might happen then.

Lizzie moved away from the fire glow and climbed up on to Scrooge's bed, which groaned and wheezed as though even her slight weight might force its collapse. She sighed, nestling down into the dusty folds of the counterpane.

'You can't sleep there,' said Sam, standing up. 'Not in his bed. He'll be back before we know it, and then what? We have to find somewhere else.'

'But . . .' she murmured, barely awake.

'Lizzie!' he hissed, tugging at her arm. 'Come on!'

Sam half dragged her from the bed and they moved towards the tall panelled door to an adjacent room. Sam expected it to be locked, and was pleasantly surprised to find that it opened with a whine and a creak when he turned the brass knob.

Scrooge must have a maid who came in while the old man was at work, Sam thought, though she clearly did not live here. Who would want to live with this old fiend? But a frugal fire glimmered faintly in the hearth and gave just enough light to see that the room was surprisingly large, with two sets of curtained windows and a large dining table and chairs.

Sam wondered why Scrooge felt the need to have such a table. He was sure that the old man never entertained anyone in these rooms. The air was musty and stale.

Lizzie headed towards the hearth and curled up in front of it like a cat. Sam found a candlestick with the greasy stub of a candle in it, and lit it from the fire. The flame's glow melted the darkness and revealed previously hidden furniture and details.

'It's nice to be inside,' said Lizzie quietly.

'I thought you was asleep,' said Sam.

'It is though, isn't it?' she said sleepily.

Sam didn't reply. Of course it was nice to be inside. Nicer than freezing your liver in some graveyard. But how were they going to ever live inside – live inside permanently – unless they did something about it? Scrooge might be their only chance. It couldn't be right for him to have all that money and them to go without.

'Tell me about the house,' said Lizzie sleepily.

'I don't remember,' said Sam.

'Yes, you do,' said Lizzie. 'Please.'

'I've told you before,' he snapped. 'There ain't no sense in talking about it. What's the point?'

Lizzie was silent for a moment, but Sam could tell the matter was not finished with. He heard her begin to sob quietly to herself.

'For God's sake, Liz,' he said. 'Don't start that.'

'It's all right for you,' she said forlornly. 'You got those memories. You can remember, but I can't. Not hardly at all. Don't be mean, Sam.'

Sam took a deep breath. Normally he would have ignored her or yelled at her, but for some reason he felt drawn to those memories when normally he avoided letting them in at all cost, because the very imagining of them cut him like a razor. The pain was all but unbearable.

'The house was by a river,' said Sam at length. 'It had dark wood weatherboard walls and a thatched roof with a big old chimney stuck through it.'

Lizzie smiled in the candlelight without opening her eyes.

'It was small but it was big enough for us,' he continued. 'It was dark inside on account of the little windows, but we was outside mostly. We was always outside. The air was clean and didn't taste of metal or coal dust when you breathed it. It felt like you was the first person ever to breathe it.

'It had a garden that went right down to the water,' he continued. 'There was ducks there and fish too. You could see pike sometimes hunting in the shadows. There was a vegetable patch where we grew our own food and you and me would hunt for caterpillars on the cabbages and we would take them in a bucket to a place well away and let them go, after making them promise not to come back.'

He paused there, summoning the courage to conjure up the next image, sun bright, blinding.

'There was a sloping grass bank and Mother used to sing to us there,' he said, his voice starting to falter. 'You on her lap and me sat alongside on a blanket. Under a big old willow tree. She'd sing and the little birds would twitter in the trees and bushes and . . .'

He stopped and closed his eyes.

'Sam?' said Lizzie.

He did not reply.

'I'm sorry, Sam,' said Lizzie. 'I shouldn't have made you remember. I know you don't like to.'

'That's just it, Liz,' said Sam. 'I love to. I love to. But I can't . . . I ain't strong enough . . .'

'Sam, I –'

Lizzie stopped and stared over Sam's shoulder with a look of utter astonishment on her grimy face. Sam frowned and turned.

The curtains were open and outside all was darkness. Out of this gloom was appearing, with horrible fluidity, the doom-laden features of Marley's ghost, floating just outside the windowpane.

Sam reeled backwards and managed to put a hand over Lizzie's mouth to stifle the scream. Marley's ghost loosened the topknot of his scarf and let his jaw flop to his chest.

'What are you doing there?' he moaned quietly, reaching out a hand towards them. 'You should not be there!'

Sam backed away some more, holding on to Lizzie

until he collided with the table. But Marley's ghost did not enter as Sam had assumed he would.

'Wait a minute,' whispered Sam. 'You ain't supposed to be here neither, are you? That's why you can't come in.'

'What do you mean?' said Lizzie. 'Do you know who that is?'

'He's called Marley,' said Sam. 'He used to work with Scrooge. When he was alive.'

'You . . . must . . . leave!' hissed the ghost angrily.

'I don't think we will,' said Sam. 'It's all right for you out there in the cold. You don't feel nothing. You're dead, ain't you?'

Marley's eyes narrowed and a curl twisted his upper lip.

'I think you may be colder than I am, by some degrees,' said Marley.

'I ain't sentimental, if that's what you mean,' said Sam. 'It's a luxury, ain't it? It's one we can't afford. So I don't care about you or your mates out there, all right?'

'You . . . must . . . leave!' he hissed again.

Lizzie whimpered.

'I don't think so,' said Sam, stepping forward and shutting the curtains.

Lizzie ran to the other side of the room, staring back towards the window, her skinny legs shaking.

'He can't get in, Liz,' said Sam.

'How do you know?' she said.

'Because if he could, he'd be in by now. He was here to tell Scrooge about them spirits, that's all. He's no more meant to be here than we are.'

'How do you know?' asked Lizzie.

Sam took a deep breath.

'I might have talked to him in the churchyard,' he said.

'What? Talked to him about what?'

'He says he's here to help save Scrooge's soul,' said Sam. 'Three spirits are coming and they're going to show the old prune the error of his ways.'

Lizzie stared at him.

'And was you ever going to tell me about it?'

Sam shrugged. Lizzie scowled.

'But he can go through walls. What's stopping him?'

'I think he's scared,' said Sam.

'Scared? What of?'

Sam shrugged and ground his teeth nervously before replying.

'I don't know. Those other spirits, I suppose. The ones who are going to teach the old man.'

It worried Sam, though he did not show it. It worried him that a phantom such as that would be scared. It made him wonder what these spirits must be like.

'Sam!' she hissed.

'Look,' said Sam, 'we're here now. It's warmer in here than out there, and old Scrooge can have his soul saved for all I care – I just want some of his loot and –'

Suddenly a bright flash burst into the room, under

the door and round the door and beaming through the keyhole. It was a blue-white light and so intense that even this edited glimpse of it dazzled their eyes.

'He's back!' hissed Sam. 'Quick – under the table!'

Lizzie needed no further encouragement and the two of them dived under the huge table, turning to peep beneath the tablecloth, which hung almost, but not quite, to the floor.

The light shone in under the door, raking across the floorboards like a lighthouse beam rakes the waves, picking out every crumb and woodlouse carcass.

And then nothing.

The afterglow still hovered in the gloom like a ghost, but the light in Scrooge's bedroom had gone out. Had he and the spirit left again?

No. Sam could hear the old miser moving about. Lizzie could hear him too and cuddled nervously into Sam, but Scrooge was climbing into bed, not coming towards them.

'What's he doing?' whispered Lizzie.

'He's going back to bed.'

'I'm so tired, Sam,' she said tearfully.

'Then go to sleep.'

'But you said I shouldn't. What if he comes in?'

'He's not coming in,' said Sam.

Lizzie turned her back on her brother and curled up prickly as a hedgehog. Sam knew to leave well alone. Lizzie would come round. She always did. Best to get some sleep.

One of the tiny fireflies of light came drifting in under the door and Sam reached out and took hold of it.

Chapter 5

The scene could not be more changed. Night was replaced by day, winter by spring. Instead of the soot and grime of the city, here was the greenery of the Kentish countryside. Here was a scene that might make a painter pause and take up his brushes.

Sam and Lizzie were standing in the garden of the house by the river, inhabiting the memory Sam had earlier described. Under the shade of a willow tree sat their mother and their younger selves.

'Are we dreaming?' said Lizzie.

'I don't know,' said Sam. 'Can we both be dreaming the same dream?'

'Mother!' shouted Lizzie. 'Mother!'

But their mother ignored them and carried on playing with the children they had been. A kingfisher flew by, a flash of turquoise blue.

'She can't hear us,' said Sam.

Lizzie shouted again.

'She don't know we're here.'

'Mother?' said Lizzie again, quieter this time.

Sam reached out and pulled Lizzie close to him.

'*Shhh*, Liz,' he said. 'She can't hear us.'

'But are we here?' said Lizzie. 'I mean, are we looking at the real world or some trick of them spirits?'

'I don't know,' said Sam. 'The real thing, I think.'

'But how?' said Lizzie. 'Why?'

Sam shrugged.

'I think maybe we've got mixed up with the magic intended for old Scrooge.'

They walked forward hesitantly. A light breeze played in the willow branches and rippled the surface of the river. Birds twittered in the bushes nearby. White clouds floated lazily in a pale blue sky.

They listened in awe to their mother talking, neither of them wishing to interrupt the magic of hearing that voice again, a voice whose notes now filled their eyes with tears. Lizzie turned to put her arms round Sam, but he pushed her away.

'This is your fault,' he said, sniffing back tears.

'What?' said Lizzie. 'What do you mean?'

'This!' he snapped, pointing to their mother and the children who hung on her every word. 'It was you, asking and asking me to tell you about her. It's you that's brought us here! The spirits must have got wind of it somehow.'

'Well, I'm glad!' said Lizzie. 'I'm glad we're here! Why aren't you?'

'Because we *ain't here*, Liz!' he yelled. 'Or we may as well not be. We can't touch her. We can't talk to her. I can't tell how I . . . I can't . . .'

His voice gave way to sobbing and he slumped to his knees. Lizzie was unmoved.

'Well, I don't care,' she said coldly. 'I'd rather stay

here like this than go back. I'd rather be a ghost here than be what we was back there.'

'We don't get to choose,' said Sam quietly, without looking up. 'Don't you understand? People like us never –'

'Sam!' hissed Lizzie.

He made no reply.

'Sam!' she repeated. 'She can see me. I mean I can see me. I can see us!'

'What are you on about?' said Sam, looking up.

But as soon as he did, he saw what she meant. Lizzie's younger self was staring at them, wide-eyed and giggling, alternately clapping her hands and pointing.

'See?' said Lizzie. 'I can see us.'

Their mother and Sam's younger self both followed little Lizzie's gaze, wondering what it was that so enthralled her, but they could clearly see nothing.

'What is it, Lizzie, dear?' said their mother with a chuckle.

'I think I can remember this . . .' said Lizzie.

'Remember what?' said Sam.

'Remember us standing here,' she said. 'Like we are now. I think I can remember this. I can remember now.'

'No, you can't,' said Sam. 'How could you? You were too little. Look at you.'

But Sam said these words without his usual certainty. He had lost all sense of what was real and what was fanciful, and Lizzie remembering was no stranger than them standing there like ghosts, looking at themselves through time. So little had seemed possible only a day or so ago. Now nothing seemed *im*possible.

Sam remembered this day too, though not for that reason. Whenever he tried to picture their early life, his mind was irresistibly drawn back to this day, this summer's afternoon. It was why he was so reluctant to talk about it with Lizzie. He knew where this memory led.

A visitor appeared beside them, as oblivious to their presence as their mother and younger selves. It was their neighbour, a busybody. Sam tried to remember her name but could not. She had some news she was clearly and obscenely eager to impart. Sam and Lizzie's father had been arrested and taken to the debtors' prison at the Marshalsea.

This was it: this was the very moment they fell into the pit.

There was a shout from the house behind them and Sam and Lizzie both turned to the sound. Confusingly, Sam was sure that the shout came from their mother, but how could it? When they turned back to her, the family was gone.

Not only that, the day was different. The white clouds overhead were replaced by grey, and the garden was wearing its dull winter colours. The river looked darkly mysterious, a joyful thing turned grim and fearsome.

They moved away through the vegetable patch

towards the house and entered through the kitchen door. They heard their mother sobbing and they saw a man standing with his back to them, their mother seated beyond, the two children at her side. The man's hair was tied in a pigtail that hung between his shoulders.

They were no longer in the cottage by the river, but in the hateful lodgings their mother had rented near the prison, rent that had taken all the money gained from pawning everything of value remaining to her.

Sam's younger self looked older than before and some of the hardness that was now such a feature of his face had taken root. Lizzie too looked less of the joyful tot she had been moments before. How much time had flown? Not more than a few months.

The greatest change had occurred in their mother though. The light had almost disappeared from her sapphire eyes, which once had evoked a summer sky and now looked like ice. Her rounded features were sunken and wan. She seemed tired and dazed, like a gin addict.

'I'm very sorry, madam,' said the man. 'I only do as I am required to do.'

'But what an occupation,' said their mother.

'It is the only one I have,' replied the man. 'We lent your husband money and he knew the consequences in not keeping up his payments to us.'

'Is that how you sleep, then?' she said. 'By reciting that tale to yourself?'

Even from behind, Sam could see the man bristle.

'I shall take my leave of you, madam,' he said. 'You must quit this house and all its contents. They will be forfeited against your husband's debt. I trust that you will find accommodation with family or friends. Good day.'

The man bowed. Their mother reached out and grabbed his sleeve.

'We have no friends,' she said. 'Nor family. This is

all my family here. We are everything to each other. Please, I beg you.'

They were to leave even that house. Their mother would live in the prison with their father, while Sam and Lizzie lived with strangers.

Sam had hoped that when their father died of jail fever, the death might free his mother from the duty she felt to be at his side. But the same fever that took him took her a week later.

And so they were alone in the world.

'Madam,' replied the man, 'there is nothing for me to do. I'm sorry.'

With that, he turned to face them. The face was younger, with a touch more colour to it, but its owner was still instantly recognisable. It was Jacob Marley.

Chapter 6

Sam and Lizzie were used to sleeping on paving slabs and iron grates and doorsteps, being moved on by constables and woken by drunks. Their sleep was normally as slight a thing as tissue paper, but this night was a soft and heavy blanket.

It was Lizzie who woke first.

'Sam!' she whispered.

Sam had no idea how many times Lizzie had said his name before he woke, rising out of the depths of sleep like a miner, blinking into the light, Marley's face still imprinted on his mind.

Voices!

'What?' said Sam, squinting into the gloom,

forgetting where they were for a moment.

Voices. There were voices in the room with them. But what was going on? The floor was cold and damp. There was earth beneath them now, not cushions as there had been. Had it all been a dream? Or did the dream, or whatever it was, continue? Sam edged towards a point in the tablecloth where it seemed to join like curtains.

'Are spirits' lives so short?' he heard Scrooge say.

'My life upon this globe is very brief,' said another voice, deep and booming. 'It ends tonight.'

'Tonight?' cried Scrooge.

'Tonight!' repeated the other. 'At midnight. Hark! The time is drawing near.'

Sam edged closer to the cloth. The deep and booming voice seemed to come from high above him. He was afraid as never before. His hold on what was real or unreal was loosening and he could not guess at the scale of whatever might greet them next. As Sam gripped the folds of the material he was surprised by the weight of it. And was that a fur trim?

'I see something strange,' said Scrooge, 'protruding from your robes. Is it a foot or a claw?'

Sam realised Scrooge must be talking about his own foot, which was sticking out from under the fur trim.

'It might be a claw, for all the flesh there is upon it,' said the booming voice. 'Look here!'

The next instant, the cloth was wrenched asunder.

Sam and Lizzie crouched, squinting and horribly revealed, like whelks pulled from their shell. They were in some terrible barren place and there stood Scrooge, trembling in his nightgown and cap.

'Spirit,' said Scrooge nervously, looking at Sam and Lizzie as though they were feral dogs, 'are they yours?'

Sam saw a giant pair of bare feet on either side of them, and then a voice boomed out above and Sam turned to see that, instead of being under the table, they were now under the heavy green fur-trimmed robes of a mighty bearded giant.

'They are Man's,' said the giant.

Scrooge stared at them incredulously.

'This boy,' said the giant, indicating Sam without looking at him, 'is Ignorance. This girl is Want. Beware them both, but most of all beware this boy, for on his brow I see that written which is Doom, unless the writing be erased.'

Sam scowled up at the giant, whom he could see now was crowned with a holly wreath that twinkled with icicles, his hair and beard grey with age.

What manner of creature was this? He looked like a forest giant, some mighty Lord of the Woods. Was he a frost giant, a King of Winter? Sam had no intention of waiting to discover what this colossus had in store for them.

Lizzie pulled him closer and she and Sam stood up, fists clenched, ready to fight their corner come what may. Punch, kick, scratch and run – that was their code and it had served them well. Scrooge spoke before they could move.

'Have they no refuge or resource?' he asked hesitantly, looking back and forth between the children and the giant.

'Are there no prisons? said the spirit. Sam grinned bitterly. The giant was feeding the old miser's words back at him. 'Are there no workhouses?'

It was as if Scrooge felt the words and the tone in which they were spoken like a slap across his face and he glanced sideways at Sam and Lizzie, though Sam could see it pained him to hold their gaze.

At first Sam thought it was the usual disgust, but now he saw it was fear. Scrooge was afraid of them. He didn't remember them from the street – he thought they were spirits too. He thought they were demons. *Maybe we are,* thought Sam. *Maybe that's exactly what we are.*

Sam looked at Scrooge's pinched pale and quivering face but felt no sympathy for him. Quite the reverse. That miserable old scrounger was getting all the attention while he and Lizzie were used like props in a pantomime. And if Marley had been involved in their family's misfortunes, then was it not likely that his partner had been too? Is that why the spirits had gathered them up?

Scrooge eyed them warily and backed away a step or two, leaving one of his slippers behind as he did so. *Well,* thought Sam with a grin, *if he thinks we're demons, then let him. It might come in useful.* He took a step towards the terrified Scrooge to try out his new-found power.

They all started, however, when the church clock began to strike. Lizzie squealed. The din was loud and mournful. The bell sounded as though it was inside their heads.

Bong. Bong. Bong.

Sam and Lizzie clamped their hands over their ears, but it made no difference.

Bong. Bong. Bong.

The sonorous clanging went on and on until at the twelfth stroke the vibrations died away and were swallowed up in a silence so profound Scrooge and the children assumed they had been struck deaf.

Suddenly Sam noticed that the giant was no longer with them. Scrooge looked about him as though the spirit might somehow be concealed behind a stone or a clump of thistles. But he seemed to have vanished.

Sam was quick to regain his wits. This was their chance. Ask the old sinner for money now and he'd give them every penny he had to get rid of them. Scrooge was so shaken he would have pulled out his own teeth if asked. It was all working in their favour. Sam just needed to figure out where they were.

But as Sam was thinking this he became aware of something moving in the darkness. Lizzie whimpered and Scrooge stared in horror as Sam turned to see a tall, black-robed and hooded figure, a depthless shadow where the face should have been.

Not something moving *in* the dark, but darkness

moving of itself. It slid noiselessly towards them, floating on a shimmering bed of mist. Sam felt his stomach drop like a stone. Lizzie tried to scream but nothing emerged save a faint hiss.

'Am I in the presence of the Ghost of Christmas Yet to Come?' said Scrooge, his voice trembling along with his shaking legs.

Sam was impressed the old man could speak at all. The Inquisition with all their thumbscrews could not have pulled words from Sam's mouth. The black spirit made no reply. All it did was raise its bony arm and point.

'You are about to show me shadows of the things that have not happened, but will happen in the time before us,' said Scrooge. 'Is that so?'

Lizzie whimpered again as the tall, cowled figure seemed to bow slightly in agreement, its flowing black robes rippling as it moved. But the phantom did not speak. It just seemed to study Scrooge with its faceless face.

This unnerved Scrooge even more. He cried out, saying he feared this spirit above all the others, and Sam could believe it was true. How could anything be worse than this? It made Marley's ghost seem almost comical in comparison. There was a pitilessness in that melancholy figure, the like of which Sam had never encountered. It was like looking into the end of the world.

'Will you not speak to me?' pleaded Scrooge.

But it was clear that the spirit would not or could not talk. The hand and its long bony finger pointed away.

'Lead on!' said Scrooge. 'Lead on! The night is waning fast, and it is precious to me, I know. Lead on, Spirit!'

The spirit began to move once more, sliding effortlessly across the frozen ground, blacker than the night, a moving shadow. It slid between Scrooge and Sam, and as it passed Sam felt the robes brush against his hand and he felt pulled along with it.

The next moment all was darkness.

Chapter 7

Sam looked for Lizzie but could not find her. The darkness of that terrible beshadowed hooded emptiness seemed to have enveloped them. He turned and turned and turned but saw nothing, fumbling his way as though a great cloak had been thrown over him.

Then, all at once, the black curtains parted and Sam saw that he was standing in a busy street under a cloudy sky. Beside him stood the hooded spirit.

'Where's Liz?' said Sam. 'Where's Lizzie? What have you done with her?'

The spirit was no more forthcoming with Sam

than it had been with old Scrooge. By way of reply, it simply raised its robed arm and pointed its finger at the other end of the street.

'What is this place?' said Sam. 'Where are we? Where's Lizzie?'

The street was heaving with people, men and women, young and old. They shouted and jostled. Sam knew the grim building towering above them – it was Newgate Prison.

The street was wet from a recent downpour. The slippery stones shone like the scales of a reptile, reflecting the glowering sky, as Sam and the spirit followed through the crowd.

Beside the prison was a wooden platform not unlike a stage, though it was a cheerless venue for a play. Near that, set into the wall, was a door, heavy and studded. As Sam tried to make sense of it, the door burst open and a group of people began to walk through. He wondered what the crowd were going to make of seeing a boy and a hooded phantom passing among them, but the crowd paid no heed at all.

Just as he and Lizzie had gone unseen by all but Lizzie's younger self, so here Sam and the spirit were invisible to this baying rabble.

Then Sam saw Lizzie. She was at the front being shoved back and forth as the crowd ebbed and flowed. She almost fell to the ground at one point and he reached out to help her, but his hand passed straight through hers.

'Liz!' shouted Sam. 'Liz!'

Neither Lizzie nor any of the group reacted to his call. Why was Lizzie here among this rabble? Why was she here without him? She never went anywhere without him and would never have come here, to a place like this, even with Sam. neither had any stomach for this kind of entertainment.

What was it Scrooge had called them? Shadows. *Shadows of the things that have not happened, but will happen in the time before us . . .*

So Sam was looking at the future. This was a glimpse into tomorrow – or at least one of the tomorrows to come. The thought of it sent a shiver through Sam's innards.

The crowd cried out and surged forward as a boy was brought out, his wrists bound and his arms gripped by guards. The guards pushed the people back and scuffles broke out. A gap opened up and Sam's view opened up. The boy being led out looked straight at Sam as though expecting to see him there, and then looked away. Sam stared back and looked into his own face.

Lizzie screamed when she saw him come out of that door and had to be stopped from running to him. A man scaled the steps and inspected the thick hemp noose that now hung from the beam above the platform.

The other Sam cried out when he saw the noose and pushed back against his guards. He got no sympathy from them or the small crowd by the platform. Only Lizzie wept as he was pushed up the wooden steps towards the hangman.

'No!' murmured Sam as he saw the shadow of himself shoved towards his fate – their fate.

The hangman asked if he had anything to say but the other Sam could only howl and whine like an animal, tears streaming down his face, snot from his nose, his mouth twisting into a dozen shapes and his eyes alternating from tight shut to bulging despair.

The horror of seeing himself so reduced was almost as terrible as seeing the dangling noose. Sam saw himself broken, wretched, crippled by fear and self-pity.

The hangman put the ragged noose round the other Sam's throat and tightened the huge knot against the back of his neck. A parson standing on the platform began to read from the Bible, his eyes and heart closed to Sam's suffering. His voice sounded bored, trembling on the edge of a yawn.

A filthy cloth hood was placed over the other Sam's head.

'No!'

The hangman walked to the side of the stage and, while the crowd murmured, he grabbed hold of a lever with both hands. Sam could see the hood billowing rhythmically with the short breaths from his future self.

After what seemed an age, the hangman received a nod from a tall, smartly dressed man below, and he pulled with all his might.

'No!'

A trapdoor opened: the other Sam dropped like a sack and was almost immediately yanked back by the noose. He cavorted horribly about for a while like a deranged puppet, and then settled to swinging gently.

He swung there, half in, half out of the hole, like a theatre trick gone wrong. All was silent save for the nautical creak of hemp rope, and then Lizzie sank to the ground in a faint and a great cheer went up from the crowd.

Sam moved to run towards her, but something seemed to hold him back. An invisible wall stood between them. He could not affect that world. Lizzie was helped to her feet and then the guards dispersed the crowd, leaving only a handful of men who stood beside the scaffold and lit up clay pipes as though they were leaning against a stall in the market.

The body had ceased to swing and hung there, grim and unmoving – as dead a thing as anything could be. For nothing is deader than a body that once had life and has it no more.

Sam stared at it, trying to take in the full sense of it, trying to restrain any attempt by his mind to imagine the face beneath that hood. Tears filled his eyes. It was some time before he could speak.

'Why are you showing me this?' he asked. 'What am I supposed to have done?'

The spirit did not reply.

'I ain't no killer,' said Sam, suddenly aware of the weight of the lead piping in his pocket.

The spirit pointed at the hanging corpse of Sam's future self.

'I ain't no killer!' repeated Sam. 'I ain't killed no one. Who am I supposed to have killed? Answer me that!'

Then all at once they were no longer in that awful place, but were instead standing outside an iron gate – a gate Sam recognised, for it was the gate to the little churchyard he and Lizzie had slept in.

But they seemed to have gone further into the future, because the churchyard was neglected and overgrown, with toppled headstones and monuments so cloaked in ivy their inscriptions could not be seen.

The spirit entered and Sam followed behind. Standing among the graves like an eruption from hell, the spirit jabbed its bony finger towards a small and neglected corner and to a modest headstone there, weathered, moss-grown, chipped.

Sam took a deep breath and leaned forward. Though he still could not read, the meaning of the letters sounded in his head as though spoken. *EBENEZER SCROOGE.* Sam knew it would be that name, but still it shook him to the marrow to see it.

'What am I supposed to do?' he said. 'You show me these things and I just have to accept their truth without a word from you. What trial have I had?'

The spirit seemed to sigh and his shoulders rose and fell and the darkness inside the hood darkened a little more.

'Look,' said Sam. 'Why torture me like this? What point is there in showing me things that I can't do anything about? What am I supposed to do? Tell me! Speak to me!'

Sam walked round and peered into the shadow in the spirit's hood where its face should have been, looking for some sign of response but seeing nothing but a deep and pitiless blackness.

'All right,' he said. 'Maybe I do kill the old man

and maybe I do get hanged for it and maybe I deserve all that I get, but what about Liz? She ain't done nothing. What happens to her? Speak to me, damn you!'

Sam grabbed hold of the spirit's sleeve and tugged on it.

'Oi!' he yelled. 'I'm talking to you! Say something, you great coal sack!'

Sam shook the spirit's robes again and saw that they were no longer standing among the graves but were in a cobbled street in the lee of a mighty railway viaduct, which arched away into the smoke-filled distance.

Chapter 8

It was dark and the nearby factory gates were closed. There had been rain here too and the lamps lit up the wet cobbles so that they glowed like hot coals. It could have been later the same day, but Sam sensed somehow that they had moved on in time.

'What's this?' he said. 'I asked what happened to Liz. What are you showing me? Does she work at that factory?'

Sam knew that factory work was poorly paid and tedious, but it would mean that she at least would be safe and might have the means to look after herself. It was something to cling to.

'Does she get work? Is this her fate? Is this where she works?'

The spirit nodded gravely and Sam smiled hopefully.

'Lizzie seems like she's weak,' said Sam. 'But she's not. She's clever. She's cleverer than me. She can read and everything. She'll be fine without me. She'll make friends. I never let her do that. I told her there was no such thing as friends on the street. But I think I was just scared she'd leave me on my own . . .'

Sam had never even thought these things before, never mind said them aloud. But as much as he tried to keep this positive feeling alive, there was something unremittingly grim about the spectre's silence.

'Please tell me she's all right,' said Sam. 'I don't mind if she works hard as long as she's safe. I could bear the horror of what I've just seen if you show me that. Just give me some sign of what happens to her.'

The spirit raised its arm and once again pointed its long finger, this time at a group of women who stood in the shadows of the railway viaduct, so cloaked in darkness Sam had not noticed them before.

'What?' said Sam. 'What should I be looking at?'

He peered at the group who, though they were not so very distant, could no more see Sam and the phantom than could the crowd at the execution.

Sam knew their kind. No one could live on the streets and not. They were streetwalkers, women who sold themselves for money to men – good, God-fearing men who went to church with their wives the following Sunday without a care.

These women dressed like actresses, their faces crusted in make-up, bold in its application to work in this low light – and to divert attention from the ravages of time and disease. And in a way, actresses were what they were, a painted smile to please the vanity of the men who used them so callously.

The coloured silks of the group flickered occasionally as they caught the light. They were like a small flock of parrots sheltering against the grey and hostile London weather.

Sam heard a noise in the distance and the group of women peered out expectantly. A hansom cab clattered down the street and pulled up alongside. A woman came out from the shadows, hands on hips, and talked to the passenger, who reached out a kid-gloved hand and, in mirror to the spirit's own gesture, pointed a long finger into the group.

The woman nodded and put out a hand, into which was placed some coins. The woman hissed and made frantic beckoning movements. Sam's mind ran ahead of events and it felt as though the ground opened up beneath him and he was falling, falling, falling. And yet he remained at the spirit's side and looked on.

From out of the group came a small figure, hesitant, reluctant. It was Lizzie, as Sam knew it would be. She was recognisable beneath her gaudy costume by the way she shuffled forward. A little older, but Sam would have recognised her anywhere.

'Please,' said Sam. 'This is worse than the last. Worse by far. Take me back there rather than keep me here to see my sister brought so low. Please. Hang me again! Hang me a thousand times rather than show me this!'

The spirit remained as inscrutable as ever. The cab door was opened and the passenger held out his gloved hand to help Lizzie inside. Once she was aboard, the door closed with a thud and the cab clattered away.

'No!' yelled Sam.

He hung his head and sobbed bitterly. His legs would no longer hold him and he slumped against the wall, pushing his face into his knees and sliding sideways into a heap on the pavement.

It took many minutes for Sam to collect himself enough to talk, wiping his face on his sleeve and looking up at the spirit who towered above him still.

'So I go to the gallows knowing that this is to be Lizzie's fate,' he said bitterly. 'Is this her death I'm looking at? Or her life? And which is worse?'

As always, the spirit remained silent. Sam shook his head.

'It's not fair,' he said. 'If I'd known this would happen, I never would have done it. Listen to me – I'm talking about something I haven't even done yet!'

But in truth Sam knew that he was Lizzie's only protector and yet he had still planned the old man's death. He was only being shown things he might have known had he but chosen to think it through.

'Look, I'm not the same as I was before,' said Sam. 'I don't want to kill him now. I swear. I couldn't do it. If I ever could, I couldn't now.'

The spirit looked unmoved. What was it old Scrooge had said? Shadows of things that will happen . . . But were they inevitable?

'Wait,' said Sam. 'Are these things set in stone? Are they what *will* be or what *may* be?'

The spirit turned its hollow hood to face him. Was there some hint of humanity in its shadows?

'Is it too late?' said Sam, grabbing the spirit's robes in both hands. 'Is it too late to change what's supposed to happen? Can I save Lizzie?'

The spirit said nothing.

'You don't have to save me,' said Sam. 'I'll go to the gallows if I have to, but just say there's some way that Lizzie can be all right. Please!'

The spirit pointed down the street to where the cab had disappeared. But the hand seemed less rigid than before, less judgemental.

'Give me another chance,' said Sam. 'Give Liz another chance. Give old Scrooge another chance for all I care. He probably deserves it too. I won't kill him and I won't hang for it and Liz won't suffer for it. Maybe he can be a better man from now on. I don't know. Look, please, I'm begging you.'

Sam sobbed and took hold of the phantom's bony hand and held it against his face, and all at once the spirit disappeared and Sam found himself back under the table with Lizzie asleep beside him.

Chapter 9

Sam looked out from under the tablecloth, half expecting it to be the robes of the giant once again. But no, it was a tablecloth and nothing more. The room was dull and ordinary, as it had been when they first entered. It was as it must have been every day – dusty and neglected. There was not the least sign that it had ever been home to magic. Or so he thought at first.

'Sam?' said Lizzie, waking up. 'What's happening? I had a nightmare.'

'*Shhh*, Liz,' said Sam gently, putting his arm round her. 'It's all right. You're with me now. Sweet Lizzie.'

Sam kissed her on the forehead and held her tightly, tears springing to his eyes as he did so. Lizzie returned his embrace and when they parted she searched his face, looking for some explanation for this change in him.

'Sam? What's happened?'

'I'm sorry, Liz,' he said. 'Sorry I . . . I . . .'

Lizzie hugged him again, even tighter.

'It doesn't matter,' she said. 'We'll always be together, won't we?'

Sam sobbed into her shoulder.

Lizzie gasped. 'There's someone there!'

She was right. Sam's eyes had not yet adjusted to the gloom, and so he did not at first appreciate that what he took to be some large piece of furniture at the other end of the room was in fact the spirit they had encountered earlier with Scrooge on that barren wasteland.

'It's the giant,' he whispered.

'I am the Ghost of Christmas Present,' said the giant. 'You have travelled with the Ghost of Christmas Yet to Come.'

Sam nodded solemnly.

'What does he mean, Sam?' said Lizzie, then dropping to a whisper she added, 'And why doesn't he look so old now?'

Sam saw that she was correct. The giant's hair and beard were no longer grey but a lusty chestnut brown, and his muscular body was evident beneath his robes, which were open a little to reveal a broad and hairy chest. His face was ruddy and he seemed to glow like a fire. Where he had once looked like a King of Winter, he now seemed to be a guardian of life in winter's death.

'You have been educated by your journey with the spirit?' asked the Ghost of Christmas Present.

'Yes,' said Sam. 'I have.'

The giant smiled weakly.

'But where are we now?' said Sam. 'You are younger than you were. How come you're still here, then? Shouldn't your turn have been done?'

The giant smiled.

'We are in the workings of Time here, Sam,' said

the spirit. 'We are behind the clock face, lad. We are among the cogs. We are in the was, is and will be all at once.

'Scrooge is with my fellow spirit, glimpsing scenes from the years yet to come, as you have done. Like you, he will see things that will reach into his very soul.'

Sam's throat dried at the thought of what he had seen and he felt the hemp against his neck once more and shuddered.

'What does he mean?' said Lizzie. 'You've been here all the time, haven't you? Sam, wait . . . my nightmare. There was a tall man in a black robe that came and . . . Oh, Sam, what's happening?'

'It's all right,' said Sam. 'We have to go.'

'Can we?' She grabbed his arm. 'All these ghosts are giving me the creeps. No offence,' she added, looking at the giant.

He laughed a great booming laugh that shook the windows in their frames.

'None taken.'

'Come on,' said Sam. 'Scrooge'll be back before we know it.'

'And you leave empty-handed?' cried the spirit. 'There is none shall stop you. Scrooge is not here and I shall not stand in your way. Does the old man's wealth not make you angry?'

'No,' said Sam. He smiled to find that it was true.

'But why should this old miser have all that money and you go without?' said the giant. 'Is it fair?'

Sam felt he was being mocked and some of his resentment returned.

'It's still not fair!' he said angrily. 'You ain't going to say it is! But I'll not be the one to take it from him, whether he deserves it or not.'

The giant nodded slowly. Sam calmed himself once more and spoke quietly now.

'I ain't never going to think well of that man,' said Sam. 'No one cares about him. No one likes him. No one would miss him if he was gone.'

'You know this for a fact?' said the giant. 'What about the man he employs?'

'Ha! The man he pays a pittance to, no doubt,' said Sam, 'and threatened to fire on Christmas Eve? The man he keeps like a dog? You're telling me that he gives a toss about that old weasel?'

'Come,' said the giant, holding out his hand. 'Let us see. Let's visit Cratchit the clerk. Or dare you not be proved wrong?'

'Sam?' said Lizzie nervously.

'All right,' said Sam, rising to the challenge. 'Let's have a look.'

Sam and Lizzie reached out together and touched the giant's robe. The next instant they were standing in a poorer part of town outside the Cratchits' four-roomed house, the giant Ghost of Christmas Present illuminating the scene with a curious flaming torch he held in his hand.

The giant shook the torch and shining droplets rained down on to the humble dwelling. The building seemed to grow a little at this blessing and the street to brighten.

'What is that, sir?' said Lizzie. 'That stuff what comes from the torch?'

'It is the essence of joy and good fellowship,' said the giant. 'Only a very small amount is needed.'

'You can make people happy and friendly, then?'

The giant shook his head.

'I remind them of the happiness and friendship they had forgotten,' he said. 'That is all.'

'Pah!' said Sam. 'What good is there in feeling happy one day if you go back to how you were the next?'

'What harm is there?' said the giant.

Sam scowled but did not reply.

The giant walked towards the house and the children held on to his robes and were, like him, magically carried inside, the giant bent double and filling half the room, unseen by all but Sam and Lizzie.

The Cratchits did not see the spirit's torch but they

felt its glow and the whole house was infused with a joy that belied its meagreness. Even Sam could feel the warmth.

They beheld a scene of cheerful chaos as the family tended to the coming meal. The eldest son, Peter, was in charge of a pan of potatoes as the two youngest Cratchits ran in yelling that they had stood outside the baker's and smelled the goose in the oven and were as sure as sure could be that it was definitely the Cratchit goose they smelled.

Bob Cratchit and his invalid son, Tim – Tiny Tim they called him – were not present and Mrs Cratchit wondered aloud what might be keeping them as the lid on the potatoes rattled and hissed.

And at that moment Martha, the eldest daughter, arrived to much excitement. She was a maid and had spent the morning cleaning and washing up after her mistress's Christmas Eve feast, whilst her mistress had urged them all wearily to clean 'a little more quietly, for heaven's sake'.

'Never mind!' said Mrs Cratchit, kissing her daughter. 'So long as you are come!'

Her mother told her to get warmed by the fire but the children saw their father coming and told her to hide, which she, good sport that she was, dutifully did.

Bob Cratchit entered, Tiny Tim on his shoulder, the little boy holding a wooden crutch, his leg girded with an iron frame. Bob noted the absence immediately.

'Why, where's our Martha?'

'Not coming,' said Mrs Cratchit.

Bob's face fell.

'Not coming?' he said. 'On Christmas Day?'

The sudden decline in Bob's spirits was too much for Martha to bear and she jumped out from her hiding place, throwing her arms round her father's neck. Lizzie chuckled at the sight, but Sam shook his head.

'Look at them,' he said. 'What is the point of all this? They are no better off today than they were yesterday, and yet they go on like they've come into a fortune.'

The festivities began full force. The feast was prepared. The goose was fetched and hailed with such respect it might have been the Queen herself. Sam smiled at the excitement that such a modest bird produced in the Cratchit household.

Peter mashed the potatoes without mercy whilst Mrs Cratchit made the gravy, and Belinda, the second eldest of the daughters, made the apple sauce. The youngest children noisily set the table and dragged chairs into place, and Bob and Tim occupied the corner of the table together.

Sam listened to Lizzie laughing and wondered why the spirit's incense had not worked its magic on him. Was he so dead to joy? Had he so totally forgotten what happiness was? He felt a kinship with the invalid Tim. *That is what I must be like inside*, thought Sam. *And yet still he tries to match the others for happiness.*

Sam had barely taken his eyes off Bob's frail son,

as he hopped unsteadily about the room, his crutch clunking against the floor as the others either steered clear of him or guided him to safety.

Bob rarely left the boy's side and Sam noticed that they were almost always in physical contact, as they were then at the table, Bob's own skinny hand seeming to be full of health and vigour beside the pale and limp, fragile hand of his son.

Everyone saw this favouritism and all knew the sad truth it concealed and none would ever have been jealous of it nor ever remarked upon it.

When Mrs Cratchit began to carve the goose and the full aroma of it was released, the younger Cratchits beat the handles of their knives on the table (which bore the bruises of earlier such beatings) and even Tiny Tim joined in with a barely audible 'Hurrah!'

The goose was consumed with a joyful enthusiasm, the eating punctuated by sighs and exhalations. With a great deal of assistance from the generous portions of potatoes, stuffing and apple sauce, it proved to be big enough to feed the whole family.

The pudding was fetched and, though not as large as it might be, was treated with all the ceremony a pudding ten times the size – and with a great deal more fruit – might have been expected to receive.

The dishes were cleared away and the fire built up so that chestnuts might be roasted, and there never could have been a rosier scene as apples and oranges were brought out to excited cries.

But Sam saw only Tiny Tim, whose eyelids were drooping now, exhausted by the activity, nestling into his father's chest, ear to his father's heart.

'Mr Scrooge!' said Bob Cratchit, standing and raising his glass for a toast, making Tim jump. 'I give you Mr Scrooge, the Founder of the Feast.'

His enthusiasm was not reciprocated.

'Founder of the Feast indeed!' said Mrs Cratchit. 'I wish I had him here. I'd give him a piece of my mind to feast upon –'

'My dear,' said Bob, 'the children. It's Christmas Day.'

Mrs Cratchit made it very clear what she thought of the notion of toasting such 'an odious, stingy, hard, unfeeling man' as Scrooge, and Sam looked up at the spirit.

'Seems like your magic is wearing off,' he said. 'Why Bob wants to toast the miser, I'll never know, but his family see him for what he is, that's for sure.'

'And yet they toast him still,' said the spirit.

It was true. The family did – for Bob's sake – toast Scrooge, however reluctantly. Sam shook his head as even Tiny Tim proffered a weak toast to his father's employer.

'Look at him,' said Sam. 'Poor little so-and-so. What's he got to toast anyone about?'

'He does it for love of his father,' said the spirit.

'Then his father's a fool to make him,' said Sam. 'And he's a fool to do it.'

The Ghost of Christmas Present made no reply.

And in his heart Sam knew he did not believe Bob Cratchit to be a fool at all, but a good man who deserved better. He wished they could do more than sprinkle fairy dust on their lives. What good was that to Tiny Tim?

'Spirit,' said Sam after a pause, trying to sound nonchalant, 'will that boy live?'

'Sam,' said Lizzie, 'don't . . .'

'Why do you care?' said the spirit.

'I just do, all right,' said Sam.

'If all remains the same,' said the spirit, 'then no – the boy will die . . . and soon.'

Lizzie began to sob.

'Why do you have to spoil everything, Sam?' she said.

'And will they stay the same?' said Sam, ignoring her.

'I cannot say,' said the spirit. 'But you see that if a man like Scrooge cannot be changed, then there are consequences.'

Sam looked at the family and back to the Ghost of Christmas Present.

'So all this, all this business with you and the other spirits – it's about that boy as well?' said Sam.

The giant smiled.

'It is about everyone Scrooge can affect,' said the spirit. 'If his future is changed, then so is theirs. We do not visit him because he is deserving, but because he is not. A bad man turned to good is benefit to all.'

Sam stared at the Cratchits.

'Did you show him this?' said Sam, tears in his eyes. 'Old Scrooge? Did you show him this?'

The spirit nodded.

'These very scenes,' he said.

'How?' said Sam, looking round. 'Why ain't he here, then?'

'Look harder, Sam,' said the spirit.

Sam did look harder, and realised that beside them, almost overlapping and intertwining with them, was a faint and ghostly image of the spirit, and beside him stood a faint and ghostly image of Scrooge.

'There are many presents, Sam,' said the spirit, answering Sam's confused expression. 'They line up next to each other into infinity. They are only the same for a moment. They are each of them changed by the actions we take. You and Scrooge have been shown the consequences of your life as you live it now.

'You mortals are all interlinked,' he continued with a sigh, 'though you seldom see it as anything but a burden or an opportunity for profit.'

And with that, they found themselves in Scrooge's house once more.

'We need to go,' said Sam. 'Good night to you, Spirit.'

'And to you,' said the spirit.

The giant's eyelids were heavy now and he seemed older. In the short time they had been with him he seemed to have aged twenty years or more. Sam pushed Lizzie towards the door but stopped and turned to look back.

'You called us Ignorance and Want,' said Sam. 'Well, I suppose that's who we are. I know you meant it clever, like. That Ignorance is something to be feared, especially by the likes of Scrooge. That the people they ignore will be the ones who'll rob them and worse. And you knew that he ought to fear me, didn't you?'

The spirit made no reply. Sam took the lead pipe out of his pocket and laid it down on the floorboards. Lizzie saw it and shook her head.

'Oh, Sam . . .' she said.

Sam hung his head and fought back the tears.

'That was a different Sam,' he said eventually. 'I'm not him any more. I swear, Liz.'

After a moment's hesitation she put her arms round him.

'We need to go,' she said.

He nodded. They opened the door, ran through Scrooge's bedroom, down the stairs and out into the street without a backward glance, where they stood panting.

They laughed with relief and embraced again. The cold seeped back into their bones and they set off walking, in no particular direction, but just to keep warm and to put some distance between themselves and that house. But they had barely walked ten steps when they came face to face with Marley's ghost. Lizzie squealed and hid behind Sam.

'Wait!' said the ghost.

'No!' said Sam. 'Leave us alone. We've had enough of ghosts and spirits to last a lifetime and I've seen things that would frighten even you, so out of my way!'

Marley's ghost stared at Sam and shook his head.

'Where will you go?' he said.

'What do you care?' said Sam. 'You . . . you were there. It was you who ruined our lives.'

'What?' said Marley's ghost. 'How did –'

'You sent my father to prison,' said Sam. 'You killed him and our mother.'

The ghost shook his head, confused.

'We're Sam and Lizzie Hunter!' said Sam. 'Ring any bells?'

Marley's ghost stared, wide-eyed.

'That's right!' said Sam. 'You killed our parents as sure as if you'd shot them.'

'I was the bullet, not the trigger,' said Marley's ghost. 'Your father –'

'Don't even talk about him!' yelled Sam. 'You haven't got the right!'

'Listen –'

'Come on, Liz. Don't be scared. He can't hurt us. He can't do nothing. Can you?'

Marley's ghost furrowed his brow and looked as forlorn as a tragic mask from the theatre, his great mouth gaping.

'Come on,' said Sam, and he pulled Lizzie forward, and they both stepped through the body of the ghost. It felt like stepping through a cold damp corridor filled with ice-coated cobwebs.

They emerged on the other side shivering, not just in their bodies but in their very souls. Neither Sam nor Lizzie felt inclined to look back, even when the ghost called after them, shaking his chains.

'You've seen the last of Sam and Lizzie Hunter!' shouted Sam over his shoulder, without looking round.

Sam laughed, so happy to be free of it all, and Lizzie laughed along with him. They hugged each other as they walked away, ready to take on the familiar demons of the London night.

'Sam,' said Lizzie as they passed beneath the shelter of an arcade, 'do you think that boy will live? That Tiny Tim?'

Normally such a question would have prompted a long lecture from Sam about the perils of caring for others when no one cared for them, but perhaps the magic of the Ghost of Christmas Present still lingered, because on this occasion Sam merely replied, 'I hope so, Liz. I really do.'

Chapter 10

With each step they took away from Scrooge's house, the more the night became simply just another cold and foggy Christmas Eve. Though it was a night that had set out to choke them with its icy fingers, it seemed to hold only ordinary fears.

Sam was cold but still his step was light. He felt as though the noose had been taken from his neck and that he had leapt from the scaffold into a new life. He had seen his fate and changed it. He had seen his own death and walked away.

London seemed like an old friend to Sam now, instead of a bitter enemy, and those who had known the fierce boy of the day before would have been startled by the smile he wore on his grimy face.

The children found shelter in the porch of the very church whose bells had signalled the spirits of the night, and were roused in the morning by the deacon, who wished them a merry Christmas by way of a kick and a curse. The good people of the parish didn't want to see homeless urchins on feast days. It was bad for the digestion.

Sam and Lizzie walked, blinking, into a bright Christmas morning of dazzling clarity. Sam felt hunger begin to claw at his stomach.

'What are we going to do now?' said Lizzie.

'I don't know,' said Sam. 'We'll think of something.'

Lizzie raised her eyebrows at that 'we'll'. This change in her brother was going to take some getting used to.

A baker whistled to them and gave them a loaf of bread, wishing them a merry Christmas. Lizzie laughed as Sam shook the man's hand and thanked him, and the man laughed along with her. Sam didn't seem to mind.

'Merry Christmas, Liz,' said Sam as they walked away, eating the bread.

Lizzie stopped and gave him a kiss on the cheek.

'Merry Christmas, Sam.'

They looked at each other, and all that they had lived and known seemed to pass between them in a fleeting moment. Lizzie was the first to break the silence.

'I can't stop thinking about what we saw,' she said.

'I know,' he replied.

'But I'm still glad we saw her, Sam. I'm glad we saw her talk and saw the old house and the river. I know you don't –'

'No, Liz,' he said, clasping both her shoulders and looking into her eyes. 'I'm glad too. Honest I am.'

Behind them, a butcher had opened his door to an excited, red-faced boy, who was talking so fast that the man was having trouble understanding what he was saying. The torrent of words washed over Sam and Lizzie – until the name Scrooge was mentioned and they both turned to watch.

'And you're sure Mr Scrooge told you this?' said the butcher suspiciously.

'Oh yes,' said the boy. 'He called me a fine fellow.'

The butcher arched an eyebrow. He had years of experience with Scrooge and none of them had resulted in anyone being called a 'fine fellow'.

'But what would he want with a turkey that big? There's only the one of him, and there's nothing but skin and bones on that. Maybe he meant the small one.'

'No,' said the boy. 'He was very sure about that. "Not the little prize turkey," he said. "The big one!"'

The butcher shook his head as though still not convinced he was not being lured into a practical joke.

'I'm to bring you back with me, with the turkey, and he'll give me a shilling,' said the boy.

'A shilling? Scrooge?'

'Aye. If we can get there in five minutes, he said he'd give me half a crown!'

The butcher stared wide-eyed. Sam smiled. He could see the man's thoughts as though his head were made of glass: *If Scrooge is going to give this boy a half-crown for fetching me, what will he give me for bringing the bird?*

'Well, come on then,' said the butcher, taking the turkey down from its hook and laying it in a barrow.

The boy, butcher and turkey set off for Scrooge's house, the barrow wheels squeaking away down the cobbled street. Sam and Lizzie set off after them, overtaking them easily.

They came at length to the entrance of the yard in which stood Scrooge's house, and Sam and Lizzie ducked back round the corner when they saw that Scrooge was standing on the doorstep, rubbing his hands expectantly.

If Lizzie had thought the change in Sam

remarkable, then this alteration was a thing of mythology and folklore. For there stood the crotchety old miser of the night before, sporting a giddy smile that would have marked him out as the kindest old grandfather that ever lived.

Sam and Lizzie stared at each other for a moment and then turned back to Scrooge, who patted the door knocker as though it were a faithful old horse and chattered away to it so merrily they thought perhaps he had lost his mind.

'Here's the turkey!' he cried, clapping his hands like an infant. 'Hallo!' he called, waving excitedly as the butcher and boy arrived with the cart and bird. 'Whoop! How are you? Merry Christmas!'

Scrooge danced round the cart, shaking his head at the size of the turkey and making the butcher gasp in good-humoured amazement.

'Why, it's impossible to carry that to Camden Town,' said Scrooge, paying man and boy with a chuckle. 'You must have a cab!'

A cab was found and off went the butcher and the turkey alongside him – an odd couple indeed. The sight of them made old Scrooge laugh and hold his chest with the exertion of it, chuckling at the thought of what Bob Cratchit – and all the Cratchits – would make of it.

Sam and Liz were fascinated to see what the old man would do next and they waited for him as he went inside and appeared half an hour later, clean-shaven and in his Sunday best.

Scrooge set off and Sam and Liz fell in behind him on the other side of the street. Where days before his vicious appearance had caused all who saw him to step aside, now his smile was mirrored in everyone he passed.

Several people wished him 'Good morning' and 'Merry Christmas', and on each occasion he seemed to be deeply moved by the words and stopped to tip his hat and shake their hands, much to the amuse-ment of all around.

Then Scrooge bumped into one of the charity men who had visited his office the day before and whom he had sent away so harshly. The man would clearly rather have avoided any contact, but Scrooge marched straight up to him and, after shaking his hand with a vigour that made the poor man's chins wobble like jelly, whilst apologising for his earlier disgraceful behaviour, he whispered into the man's ear. Sam could tell by the charity man's reaction that Scrooge was offering him an exceptionally generous donation.

'Lord bless me!' exclaimed the man, amazed. 'Are you serious?'

Scrooge assured him he was and would take no thanks, just an assurance from the man that he would come and see him at the office so that he could settle with him. When the man agreed, it was Scrooge who thanked *him*.

Sam and Lizzie looked on in astonishment at this behaviour. Had they not seen it with their own eyes, they would neither of them have ever believed each such a change possible.

They followed him to church, where he greeted those outside warmly despite their clear trepidation when he first approached. But so charming was this new Scrooge that no one could resist for more than a moment.

After the service he again shook every hand available to him and patted the head of every child who passed within range, and then he took himself off alone down the church steps and stood for a while, watching the people hurrying this way and that.

He wore a different expression now. It was not the excitable face of his first few infant steps along the road to generous humanity, but neither was it the scowl of old. It was a thoughtful expression, tinged with sadness as he looked from face to face.

Then, like a sailor setting out on a long journey, he entered the flow of people and wandered among them, Sam and Liz in pursuit. He looked down into the kitchens of the houses he passed and saw the servants at work on the meals, and spent time chatting to the beggars he had so often ignored in times past.

His smile had returned and this new and novel contemplation of his fellow man – this new attachment he was discovering – clearly brought him pleasure, and yet Sam could not help feeling there was something on the old man's mind.

'It's like he's looking for something,' said Sam.

'Looking for what?' asked Lizzie. She had felt it too.

'Who knows, Liz?' said Sam as Scrooge disappeared into the throng. 'Come on . . .'

Chapter 11

The extraordinary events of Christmas Eve and
Christmas Day faded more quickly than Sam or
Lizzie could have imagined. It was hard to keep firm
hold of such strangeness and soon they began to
doubt their own memories. All except – for Sam –
that glimpse of his own dreadful fate on the gallows
and of the consequences it would have for Lizzie.
The image of that carriage and the sound of its
wheels up the wet cobbles beneath the viaduct
would never leave him, however much he might have
wanted it to. It was a livid scar on his mind. Had he
done enough to assuage it or erase it? Only time
would tell.

Lizzie had never asked him what he saw that night. She knew that it must have been terrible for such a change to have been wrought in him. She did not want to know what it was, even had she believed that Sam would tell her if she asked.

Sam and Lizzie had followed Scrooge all the way to his nephew's house and had watched him pace up and down, picking up the courage to knock at the door. But he need not have feared, for the nephew was a good soul and welcomed his uncle in as warmly as if he had been expected.

They had stood and listened to the voices inside, the sudden bursts of laughter as the new Scrooge was greeted with joyful surprise by one and all. Then they had walked away, their part in the story done.

Or so they thought.

Sam was exhilarated to have a second chance and Lizzie felt as though her brother – the brother she loved – had returned to her at long last, but though their souls had been lifted, their bodies had not escaped the grip of squalor. Their circumstances were the same as before.

The warmth in their hearts was a warmth they had not had before, but it did not thaw their feet at night; it did not fill their pockets or their bellies. The magic was fading fast. Reality was stalking them like a murderer.

In his darker moments, Sam wondered what future the Ghost of Christmas Yet to Come would show him now. Had they simply exchanged one grim fate for another? Surely it must be better than the one he had glimpsed, but were they doomed no matter what?

The season of good cheer would soon be over. The bells had already rung in the New Year and it felt as always to Sam like a call to arms, like a battle about to start. But this year some of the fight in him had gone. He was a kinder person now but a softer one. He felt the cold more keenly. His war with mankind was over and he realised that it had been the fight that had kept him alive all these years.

It was Twelfth Night, the last night of Christmas, when the fabled Wild Hunt was said to ride out across the sky. It was a lively enough night for it, to be sure, with a northerly wind sending grey clouds across the sooty blackness. Was that the sound of Odin's horse rumbling across the heavens? Every crack and gap became a whistle for the wind and every shop sign creaked on its chains. Gates rattled and shutters banged.

It was a pitiless night. Sam pulled Lizzie close but they felt little warmer than the air around them. But then the cold always bit deepest when they were hungry, and they had not eaten more than scraps for days. Sam had given the better of even these few morsels to Lizzie, but she seemed to be fading like a ghost herself. She was pale and thin, and on the few occasions she spoke, her voice was so quiet it needed dead silence to hear it.

They were both fading. Their little mark upon the world was being slowly erased. Sam wondered if they would see the morning. Normally this feeling of having his toes over the edge of the grave pit would have fired him up to live in spite of everything. But much of that spark was gone.

It was time to look for shelter or die in the streets like dogs. They had found such bodies themselves in the morning – the blue, frozen corpses of those who had taken the full force of the night and been felled by it.

'Come on, Liz,' said Sam. 'We can make it yet. This way . . .'

Chapter 12

The wind was exhausting. It bellowed in their ears and blinded their eyes. They shuffled along, squinting into the gloom, their senses smothered and dulled. A cliff edge could have been three steps ahead and they would have been falling before they knew.

And so it was that Sam walked straight into a set of rusty iron gates that creaked at his touch, making a particular whine that sparked his memory.

This was the very graveyard they had slept in on Christmas Eve: the last resting place of that money-man-turned-ghost, Jacob Marley. It was here it had begun. They had come full circle, pulled back like metal to a magnet.

Sam thought about turning back, but he knew they had to find some place to sleep or they were done for. He opened the gates and they walked through, the tumble of headstones and leafless trees seeming to drift towards them through the murk.

Though they could scarcely see well enough to guide themselves through the headstones, and Sam had specifically sought to avoid it, some curious trick of fate brought them to the selfsame tombstone as before, and Sam helped Lizzie to climb inside.

Were we meant to die that night? thought Sam. *Were we meant to die that night the magic happened? Has everything since just been stolen time?*

Sam looked at Marley's headstone and had another thought. *Maybe we did die that night, after all,* he mused. *Maybe we're trapped here, doomed to repeat it all over and over. Maybe this is what haunting is. Maybe this is what it feels like to be a ghost.*

But did that mean they were doomed to repeat that whole dreadful adventure? Would Sam once more be taken to that prison yard to see his own execution? Would he see Lizzie taken away again in that cab?

As though to answer these thoughts, Sam's eyes widened as he saw something pale emerge from the earth in front of Marley's headstone. At first it was like the top of a large egg, then the back of a head with a grey pigtail, then more and more, until there was a whole man there, who turned to face him. It was Jacob Marley, of course.

So it *was* to begin again.

'No,' said Sam, tears welling in his eyes. 'I can't. I can't do it. I ain't got the strength.'

'Sam?' said Lizzie faintly. 'What is it?'

'Listen to me,' groaned Marley.

Lizzie peered out at the sound of the ghost's mournful voice.

'Leave us alone, villain,' said Sam. 'We ain't bothering no one here.'

'Sam –' began Lizzie.

'It's all right, Liz,' said Sam. 'He can't hurt you. He can't hurt anyone.'

'But, Sam,' continued Lizzie. 'Look. He's not the same. His chains are almost gone . . .'

Sam followed Lizzie's gaze and saw that Marley's chains were indeed almost gone, save for several large links still attached to his ankle. Although both links and the leg to which they were bound were translucent, Sam could see that the shackle bit deep into Marley's phantom flesh.

Clearly this was no simple repeat of the previous events. For not only were the chains all but gone, his face was no longer the terrible open-mouthed mask of before. The lower jaw that had no previous means of control, and lay on his chest unless tied in place, now did as its owner bid.

'Scrooge is looking for you,' said Marley's ghost.

'So?' said Sam. 'Let him look. We never took a thing from him. We broke into his house, but we never took a thing.'

'Scrooge does not want to harm you,' said the ghost. 'He wants to help you. *I* want to help you.'

Sam was so surprised by this remark that he jerked his head, banging his skull on the slab above it.

'Help us?' he said, wincing. 'Why would he want to help us?'

'Scrooge has lived a bitter, loveless life,' said Marley. 'Joyless as a stale pie. As I did before him. He has been shown the error of his ways. He wants to be a better man.'

'Does he now?' said Sam. 'Well, good for him. We don't need his help.'

Marley raised an eyebrow and shook his head.

'All right,' said Sam, seeing his meaning. 'We don't *want* his help.'

'You would rather die, then,' said the ghost.

Lizzie's fingertips bit into Sam's arm.

'It is a subject I know a little about,' continued Marley. 'I cannot recommend it.'

'We ain't going to die!' said Sam.

But he was not as sure as he sounded and there was something about the way Marley looked at him that made him wonder if the ghost knew something.

'We ain't going to die,' repeated Sam. 'Let him help that boy – that Tim Cratchit. Let him pay his clerk some decent money. How about that?'

'You'd put that boy ahead of your own needs?' said Marley.

'I don't know,' said Sam. 'It seems fair, I suppose. What are we to Scrooge? I suppose the boy is some way ahead of us in the queue . . .'

'Let Scrooge help you too,' said Marley. 'He has the means for both. Let *me* help you for that matter.'

'You can't help us,' said Sam. 'We saw those spirits flying around. You can't help us, you know you can't. That's part of your punishment, ain't it? For being as mean as old Scrooge there.'

'Yes,' agreed Marley, 'it is. And no, I can't help you. Not directly I can't. But I can urge you to go to Scrooge, and he can. I can help you help yourselves.'

Sam stared coldly at the spirit's face.

'You got a nerve, ain't you?' he said. 'It was down to you that we're on the streets in the first place.'

Marley lowered his head.

'That's right,' said Sam. 'Hang your head in shame. We saw you there. It's all your fault!'

'Is it?' said Marley, looking up.

'What's that supposed to mean?'

'Oh, I played my part,' said the ghost. 'I certainly played my part, and I have paid dearly for it. But I was not alone . . .'

'Look,' said Sam. 'If you've come here to curse my father then you may as well be on your way. My father was a good man.'

Marley shook his head.

'No,' he said grimly. 'No, he wasn't.'

Furious, Sam launched himself at the ghost but tumbled through his body to land sprawled on the ground, fists flailing.

'Give me one good memory you have of him,' said Marley, 'and I will take it back.'

Sam got to his feet, scowling, dusting himself off. As he did so he tried to do as the spirit asked, but found nothing. Nothing.

'You can't think of anything at all, can you?' said the ghost sadly. 'Good or bad. Either of you.'

Marley looked at Lizzie, who shook her head.

'The reason you cannot think of him is that he was never there,' he went on. 'He was a wastrel. He was a gambler and a poor one at that. I warned him many times where his actions were leading, but still he borrowed more money to throw after that which he had already wasted.

'And to make matters worse, your mother, whom he was not fit to pass in the street, loved him with a devotion that I found exasperating and saddening in equal degrees.

'I was a cool businessman and not one for senti-mentality, but your mother's case affected me and I offered her help. She refused and insisted on living with that man in the Marshalsea, a decision which cost her her life. She did, however, allow me to find somewhere for you . . .'

'Pah!' snorted Sam. 'You'll get no thanks from me for putting us up with those people. I had to get Lizzie away from there or . . .'

Again Marley shook his head.

'No,' he said. 'You chose to leave, Sam. They were strict and they were a little severe. But they were kind people and they would have looked after you.'

'No!' shouted Sam. 'They were horrible.'

Marley looked at Lizzie.

'Do you remember them, Lizzie?' asked the ghost.

'She remembers them all right,' said Sam.

But Lizzie was ignoring Sam, trying to see beyond the stories he had told about them.

'Try, Lizzie,' said Marley.

'He's right . . .' said Lizzie, struggling to recall. 'I think he's right. It was you who weren't happy there.'

'Liz,' said Sam.

But he could not argue his case. It was the truth. Sam had taken them away from that house. He could not hit out at fate and so he had hit out at these people who were trying their best to help. He had made things impossible for himself and then added to this error by making Lizzie side with him. He was the reason they were on the streets.

'You were angry, Sam,' said Marley. 'And you had every right so to be. You had the recklessness of your father but you could not leave Lizzie, for you had the devotion of your mother. We can't tell what strengths and what weaknesses we shall be gifted by our parents.'

It was Sam's turn to hang his head.

'But will you die railing against the hand you have been given, or throw in those cards for another?' said Marley. 'Will you die from stubbornness, just as it has kept you alive all these years?'

'I'm so sorry, Liz,' said Sam quietly.

'I wanted to be with you,' she replied. 'I could

never have stayed there without you. It would have broken my heart if you'd gone and left me there.'

'Sam,' said Marley, 'ask for help. It's waiting for you.'

'Why does he care about us?' Sam said. 'What about everyone else on the streets? Don't they count for nothing?'

Marley raised an eyebrow.

'I thought you didn't care about them,' he answered with a twist of his lip. 'That was a weakness, you said. A weakness you couldn't afford.'

It was Sam's turn to have his words fed back to him. They tasted bitter.

'I see what you're doing,' said Sam. 'You're trying to make me sound like him – like Scrooge – but it won't wash. He could have helped people and he didn't. We had nothing. If we didn't look after ourselves, then who would?'

Marley nodded.

'True. I cannot say that any of what you say is a lie, but where do these words lead? Things have changed. A door that was locked is now open. Are you brave enough to walk through?'

Sam looked away, muttering. Marley dropped to his knees and looked them in the eyes. Sam and Lizzie had been terrified of that face, but now it was nothing more than a sad and tired old face. There was kindness there.

'Do you think the world will care if you die?' said Marley. 'Do you think the world will notice?'

Sam did not reply. Lizzie squeezed his arm again.

'If you die from pride or spite,' said Marley, 'your father will have won. His selfishness did for his own life and your mother's. It is a miracle that he has not already done for yours. But that miracle is at an end. It is time to embrace another.'

Sam squeezed his eyes shut. Lizzie felt his pain and rested her head against his shoulder.

'All right,' he said eventually. 'All right.'

When he opened his eyes, a tear ran down each cheek, and Marley was gone.

Chapter 13

Sam lifted the heavy metal knocker and struck it three times. It seemed to echo through the house, and for the first time Sam felt afraid.

As the sound of the door knocker died away, the distant patter of footsteps came in answer and grew in volume as they descended the stairs and headed towards Sam.

The door swung open and, to Sam's amazement, instead of the dark and dismal interior that they had seen when they were last there, the hallway was now brightly lit and decorated.

Sam actually wondered for a moment whether he had the right house, particularly when he looked into the face of the man who had opened the door and saw, instead of Scrooge, his nephew, with a wide smile on his face.

'Well, now,' he said. 'What have we here?'

The young man's smile weakened as he saw Lizzie, and he stepped forward to help Sam hold her up.

'Come in,' he said. 'Come out of the cold. Uncle!'

He helped Sam and Lizzie across the hall as a group of people gathered at the top of the stairs outside Scrooge's door began to descend hurriedly.

'Oh my Lord,' said a woman, rushing to take Lizzie from Sam.

Sam struggled at first but he did not have the strength. He was about to fall, when he found himself lifted up and into the arms of Scrooge's nephew.

Lizzie was carried ahead of him and they were both taken to the room where they had hidden under the table.

It was brightly lit, with a great fire roaring in the hearth and wreaths of holly and mistletoe on the walls. The long dining table was laden with food and silverware and crystal glasses, laid out as for a feast.

Am I dreaming? thought Sam. *Am I asleep in the graveyard and dreaming? Or am I dead?*

'Bring them to the fire,' said another man, whom Sam recognised straight away as Bob Cratchit, Scrooge's clerk. 'Mind out the way, Tim, there's a good lad.'

The small boy hopped about excitedly on his crutches.

'Who are they, Pa?' he said.

'Well, I'm not sure, my boy,' said Bob Cratchit to his son.

Lizzie was put down in a chair by the fire and a blanket wrapped round her. A woman knelt next to her, rubbing her hands.

'Keep her warm, my darling,' said Scrooge's nephew, as he put Sam down in a chair on the other side of the hearth. 'Let's get them some soup, Bob. They need something warm inside them. They are so cold and I don't think they can have eaten for days. Where's Uncle?'

'I'm here, my boy,' said a voice nearby. 'I'm here, Fred.'

Sam turned at its sound and there was Scrooge. The sour, pinched old miser of a fortnight ago was now a picture of geniality.

'Upon my word!' he said. 'Upon my word! It's them. Is it really them? It is! It is!'

'You know these children, Uncle?' said Fred.

'I do,' said Scrooge. 'In a manner of speaking.'

'But how?'

Everyone in the room – the clerk, the nephew, their wives and their children, including the boy on crutches – all looked towards Scrooge for an answer.

Sam could see by the uncomfortable look on Scrooge's face that the old man had not shared the events of that night with his guests.

'Who are they, Uncle?' asked Fred.

Scrooge had no answer.

'Ignorance,' said Sam. 'My name's Ignorance. This is my sister, Want.'

Everyone exchanged puzzled looks – all except Scrooge, who smiled sadly at Sam as a maid arrived with bowls of soup.

Neither Sam nor Lizzie thought they would be able to eat and Lizzie had to be helped at first, but soon the soup worked its magic, warming their innards and dissolving the fog that still clung to their brains.

'Sam?' whispered Lizzie. 'What's going on?'

'Sam you say?' said Scrooge. 'Of course! How d'you do, Samuel! And you must be Elizabeth. Ha! Oh my word, but how the fates are playing with us all!'

'How does he know who we are?' said Lizzie.

'This is Samuel and Elizabeth Hunter,' said Scrooge to those around him. 'Ha! Who would believe it?'

Lizzie stared at Sam in confusion.

'It's all right,' Sam told her. 'Everything's all right.'

'Are they spirits?' she said, peering suspiciously at the crowd that sat watching them eat.

'No, Liz. I don't think so.'

'I've been looking for you,' said Scrooge.

'Yes, I heard,' Sam replied.

Scrooge smiled and peered at him.

'Yes,' he said. 'From our mutual friend, no doubt?'

'He's no friend of mine.'

Scrooge frowned and nodded.

'What on earth is all this about, Uncle?' said Fred. 'Is no one going to explain what's going on?'

'Well,' said Scrooge, 'why don't we all sit ourselves down and I shall try.'

The whole audience leaned in expectantly as Scrooge began his tale. He took a little while to start, his jaw and lips chewing over the words before they came out.

'Some of you remember my old partner, Jacob Marley, do you?' said Scrooge finally.

Fred and Bob Cratchit exchanged a frown. Scrooge winked at Sam and Lizzie, and so they took this cue to keep silent.

'Ha! Jacob was an acquired taste,' said Scrooge with a chuckle. 'For most it was a bitter taste they did not try again. But I liked him, though he did not want me to, I think. Admired him too, though he did not want my approval either.

'He was a good businessman and that, in those days, was everything to me. He showed me all I needed to know of the business and I was an eager student.'

Sam saw tears glistening in the old man's eyes.

'Jacob trusted more and more of the business to me and he kept only a few cases as he neared the days of his retirement. He had no family and I was both surprised and honoured to discover that he had left the business to me in its entirety upon his death.

'He was a careful investor and frugal in his own living. He had inherited a considerable fortune from his parents and seemingly did not spend a fraction of it. In fact, he seems to have taken as much pleasure in not spending his money as another might derive from a lifetime of excess.

'So Jacob died a wealthy man. On going through his effects, I discovered a curious box containing papers relating to a certain man who had failed to repay his debts or keep up the payments – a not uncommon occurrence.

'This man had been sent to the Marshalsea as a debtor and had died soon thereafter of jail fever, along with his poor wife, who had chosen to join him there.

'Jacob was a man whom I had thought was hardened to the work we did, and yet this case had clearly affected him. It had eaten away at him for all those years. He had tried to find the children of that sorry couple: Samuel and Elizabeth – these children you see here.'

'What?' said Sam. 'The living Marley?'

Scrooge nodded.

'What does he mean by that?' whispered Mrs Cratchit to her husband. 'The *living* Marley?'

'*Shhh*, my dear,' said Bob. 'Let Mr Scrooge continue.'

'Marley had tried to find them,' Scrooge went on, 'and help them – to try to make some recompense for the savage blow that had been dealt them. But he failed.

'He had placed them with friends, but the children had run away. He tried every avenue, every poorhouse, but without any luck. They had disappeared from the face of the earth, and Jacob was left with the guilt of it, wondering what terrible fate had befallen them.

'I confess I was a little bemused by the discovery of a soft heart beating in the chest of my codfish of a partner, but I decided that I would honour his intentions and place his savings and the moneys from the sale of his effects into a trust on their behalf.

'I do not think I ever expected that these children would come to claim it – how could they, not knowing its existence? – but it felt wrong to reallocate it against Jacob's wishes.'

'It sounds as though you had a softer heart than you would have admitted to, even then, Uncle,' said his nephew with a smile.

This was answered with another twinkle of tears from the old man.

'I wish I could say that was true, Fred,' said Scrooge seriously. 'I really do. But I was lost. Utterly lost. I made no attempt to find them. Until now . . .'

'But I don't understand,' said his nephew. 'If Jacob had tried and failed to find them, how did you succeed? How did you know where to look, and what brought them to your house?'

Scrooge smiled at Sam and Lizzie.

'I think a mutual friend must have told these children of my search.'

Sam nodded.

Everyone in the room looked more mystified than before the tale was begun, and Fred shook his head in puzzlement. What 'mutual friend' could a man like Scrooge have with urchins like these? But Fred was so very pleased with the change that had come over his uncle that neither he, nor anyone else, wished to question any part of it too intently for fear of breaking the spell.

'You are – or you will be – very wealthy indeed,' said Scrooge to Sam and Lizzie. 'You are too young yet to inherit the money but –'

'Wealthy?' said Lizzie. 'Us?'

Scrooge grinned and nodded.

'I swear it!'

'Well, wealthy or not,' said Fred's wife, 'these children need a bath and those clothes need burning. Lord knows what wildlife they have brought with them. Will you help me, Mrs Cratchit?'

'Happily, ma'am,' said Mrs Cratchit, who had been furtively scratching for the last ten minutes.

Despite all Sam and Lizzie's protestations, water was boiled, a tub and soap were fetched and the two of them were scrubbed one after another, Lizzie by the women and Sam by Bob and Fred.

Their clothes were indeed thrown on the fire – and a terrible stench they made in the burning. Mrs Cratchit and Fred's wife were sent off in search of new clothes and they returned in an hour with some items borrowed from friends with children of a similar size. The children when they reappeared were all but unrecognisable as the grubby waifs who had entered the house hours before. The faintest trace of colour was even appearing in Lizzie's face. Sam's expression was still far from cheerful, however.

'I sense some unease,' said Scrooge. 'I had thought you might be more excited to discover you were to become a man of means.'

Sam took a deep breath and let it out falteringly.

'I suppose I don't feel like I deserve it,' he replied.

'Did you think I deserved the money I had?' said Scrooge. 'Or Marley? Honestly?'

'No,' said Sam.

Bob Cratchit's eyes widened.

'Ha!' said Fred with a hearty chortle.

Scrooge chuckled merrily and Sam, despite himself, joined in. Lizzie laughed and so did Tiny Tim, who had sat himself down nearby to marvel at these new visitors. The other Cratchit children settled down beside him.

'Then do something to deserve it, boy,' said Scrooge. 'Use your money well. Money can be used for good, you know. I realise you have every reason to believe otherwise, but it can.'

'Uncle is right, lad,' said Fred. 'I myself am involved in many schemes to help the poor and the working man.'

'And the working woman, my dear,' said his wife.

'Of course,' said Fred.

Sam looked from face to face until he reached Lizzie's, and then he closed his eyes and nodded.

'I will,' he said. 'I will use it for good. I swear. All of you can hold me to it.'

Tiny Tim clapped his hands at this thought. He seemed eager to ensure that Sam kept his word and Sam laughed – which only made him clap all the more excitedly.

'But you will not inherit the money for a while,' said Scrooge. 'And until you do . . .'

'Yes?' said Lizzie, a worried look on her face.

'Until then, I should like you to live here with me.'

Sam and Lizzie stared at him in wonder.

'If, of course, you would like to,' he added.

Sam and Lizzie looked around at the room: the fire raging in the hearth, the choir of smiling children's faces, the kindly twinkle in Scrooge's eye.

'Yes!' said Sam. 'I mean, please, sir. Yes.'

Lizzie jumped to her feet and threw her arms round the old man's neck, making him splutter and huff most comically. Everyone in the room laughed once again.

'Bless you!' said Lizzie.

'God bless us, every one!' said Tiny Tim.

And Sam, not known for such displays, went over and embraced the old gentleman himself, and when he did, it felt like a great weight had dropped from him all at once, for until then he had not understood how very heavy hate can be.

Epilogue

Now we must travel years ahead, since we, like spirits, can move through time in our imaginings. We find ourselves once more outside Scrooge's house, although it is a house much changed in the interim.

Snow is falling and the street is thick with it, but the dark and foreboding house of old has been cleaned and given a new suit of paint, with a shining front door of holly green on which the curious old brass knocker still hangs. This door knocker was the one thing Scrooge insisted must remain unchanged when he bought the whole building and had it renovated.

Opening the door we find it is Christmas once

again, but a Christmas a dozen years hence. The hall is decked in holly and ivy and a colossal Christmas tree pokes its way upwards towards the skylight above the stairwell.

We can hear children's voices echo around those walls – walls so long starved of such delights. For a house can starve as well as any man or woman, child or babe in arms, if love is denied it.

But this love-starved place has been reborn. The word 'merry' could never have been associated with the Scrooge of old, but this house could be an illustration to the word in a dictionary. It is a veritable Christmas card, and we now step into it.

People who shunned this house in earlier times long for an invite to one of the many parties held here through the year, and everyone agrees that no more hospitable a household exists in all London.

The owners of the childish voices come giggling and scampering down the stairs. They cannot see us. We walk unseen as though we too are brought here by spirits, and they run through our bodies as through mist.

The door opens behind us and Sam enters. He is a man now, grown to his full height with a handsome face, broader than it was and, though older, softer in its features.

His expression, as he walks in, is thoughtful, haunted by a trace of sadness. He has been to visit Jacob Marley's grave, as he does every Christmas Day (and many days between). The headstone is clean now and a rose grows where nought but moss and nettles were to be seen.

Sam has not seen Marley's ghost again, but this has been a source of happiness rather than regret, because he knows that this must mean his benefactor finally found peace and sleeps soundly now, untroubled by spirits or guilt.

Sam has no religion, though he tried so as to please Lizzie and Scrooge. He has no belief in heaven, but knows that Marley suffered a kind of hell before his release. He has no explanation for the wonders he experienced, but he embraces the mystery as a friend.

What forces were at work that Christmas Eve he cannot guess, but he felt something old moved among them – something that went back well before these houses and streets and churches were built.

Sometimes he thinks it was the combined yearnings of them all, conjuring up these spirits to be the means of their own salvation. Mostly, he just accepts his new fate gratefully, and does not think of the fate he dodged or the means of its avoidance.

Scrooge was good to his word and they lived happily with him for many years. Sam still lives here with Scrooge and declares that he has no intentions of living anywhere else. No son and father could be more devoted to each other than Sam and Scrooge.

Scrooge himself taught Sam to read and, more than that, showed him the power of books to mould a man and to shape the imagination. Sam's world grew and grew with each book he finished.

He inherited his fortune and was shocked to discover just how wealthy he had, that instant, become. But he too was true to his word and set about, from that day, putting the money to some good.

With help from Scrooge and Fred, Sam has supported charities that help the homeless and the destitute. With their assistance he has, moreover, set up an institute – the Marley Institute – that contains a lending library and provides courses for the education and advancement of the poor.

Carved in Portland stone above the door are the words: *Ignorance and Want: beware them both, but beware Ignorance most of all.* A vicar from the nearby church enquired as to what text Sam had taken these words from.

'Experience,' he answered, much to the bemusement of the vicar.

Now Sam climbs the stairs and his mood is lifted at each step as he hears the happy, familiar voices of those who were witness to the transformation of his fortunes and have been such steadfast friends ever since.

Here is Lizzie, now twenty years old, grown into beauty, which she wears with a light and easy charm. She stands beside her husband, a lawyer who lives in chambers nearby. He is a good man, a little nervous still of the family all about him. He sees how she looks at the children and catches her eye, making her blush.

Here is Fred, Scrooge's nephew, whose laugh could match the Ghost of Christmas Present's for volume and jollity. He never lost faith in his uncle and loved him despite receiving little by way of affection in return. Scrooge has done his level best to make reparation for this failing in the years since the visitation of the spirits, and everyone remarks on how close they are as uncle and nephew.

And Fred's wife, who despaired of Fred's soft-heartedness towards Scrooge, now loves the old man as much as he. Here she sits with their son and daughter, playing a little harp and singing them a song.

Here is Bob Cratchit, looking a little fuller in the figure than the man he once was. Here are his wife and his children, all grown up now – Martha and Belinda with husbands and children of their own. Peter is in the navy and stands in his uniform, home from the wars. The two smallest are now as tall as their father, their taste for mischief undiminished.

Here, especially, is Tiny Tim, the sickly boy whose life would surely have been forfeit had not Scrooge seen the error of his selfish ways and taken a special interest in his fortunes. No one would have dared to believe it possible that he might be here yet, standing among them still – not rude of health, but far from the sickly lad he was.

Sam has been like an uncle to the boy and a kindly one at that, despite the fact that he is only a few years older than Tim himself. But Sam's experiences have made him older than his years. Even Fred defers to him occasionally. Tim is the only one who can ever persuade Sam to talk about his life on the streets, and when he does, Tim sits in rapt attention, like a snake to a charmer's flute. And the reason Sam will tell him the stories is because he knows that Tim sees them not as entertaining anecdotes, but for what they are – searing hot coals pulled from the terrible furnace of Sam's memory. Tim knows the pain and because he knows the pain, he helps to heal it.

Only one chair in the room remains empty, next to the fire. It is the chair old Scrooge occupied that night the spirits came, and though he exchanged most of his drab old furniture for new, the old man kept this chair as a reminder of how low he had once been. Sam and Lizzie look towards the chair in memory of that night.

But fear not, here comes Scrooge now, a smile on his lips. The old man is with us still and seems, if anything, more sprightly than he did all those years ago when lovelessness had crooked his back and pinched his face. There are more lines on that face than before, but they track the passage of smiles and laughter now.

He holds a book in his hand and sits down, a mischievous twinkle in his eye. He looks up at Sam, who smiles back, taking a seat with all the others. An expectant hush greets the opening of the book, as the candlelight flickers over the gilt embossed letters on the cover. Scrooge always reads them a ghost story on Christmas Eve. It is a tradition and a fine one at that.

For what would Christmas be without a ghost story?

Chris Priestley on A Christmas Carol

A *Christmas Carol* was read to me by a teacher when I was about eight. It was the 1960s and my father was serving in the British Army, and we were stationed in Gibraltar. We lived in an apartment with a balcony that looked out across the Mediterranean to the Atlas Mountains of Morocco. It was far removed from the Victorian London setting of *A Christmas Carol*, with its freezing fog and dark cobbled streets, but I think it struck me all the more powerfully there, separated as I was from the snowy *olde worlde* Christmas I imagined back in England. It was about this time that I remember telling my teacher that I wanted to be a writer when I grew up.

Dickens certainly played his part in that wish. *A Christmas Carol* has one of the best opening lines in literature. 'Marley was dead: to begin with.' Who would not want to carry on reading after that? It is full of wonderful descriptions: Scrooge's house looked as though 'it must have run there when it was a young house, playing at hide-and-seek with the other houses, and forgotten the way out again.'

Dickens' voice is there too – boldly, as though telling you the story personally. Scrooge is as close to the first spirit 'as I am now to you, and I am standing in the spirit at your elbow.' Yes, Dickens can be horribly sentimental and that tendency is much in evidence here, but he has also tempered the text with a fierce sense of injustice and a clear desire to put the frighteners on his audience. Because *A Christmas Carol* is a ghost story. Or at least it is a story with ghosts. But is it scary?

Well, I remember being deliciously disturbed by Marley's Ghost, rising up from the cellar with his clanking chains. When I heard the description of that scarf being untied, my heart sank as swiftly and as surely as Marley's jaw does when it drops to his chest, his mouth gaping open like a grave. But *A Christmas Carol* reaches a new level of dread when it reaches the section with the silent, cowled figure of the Ghost of Christmas Yet to Come. He is often seen as Death, because he shows Scrooge his own grim and friend-less end, and I am struggling to see where that black-hooded Death figure that so haunts our imagin-ation ever appeared before *A Christmas Carol*.

The same can be said of the giant Ghost of Christmas Present who seems more Bacchus than Santa Claus, and yet is clearly a stage on the route to the jolly, red-faced Father Christmas figure we know so well. But even he is not without threat, as the feral children Ignorance and Want emerge from under his robes. Children always relate to other children, and I remember finding them particularly disconcerting. I remember the spirit's words – as true now as they were when Dickens wrote them – telling Scrooge to 'beware them both' but to beware Ignorance most of all.

Dickens alerted me to social injustice. When the charity men ask him for money, Scrooge asks if the workhouses are still in operation. When they say that they are but many would rather die than go there, Scrooge replies, 'They had better do it, and decrease the surplus population.' Scrooge is not just a grumpy old rogue, he is 'hard and sharp as flint'. Dickens pulls no punches in making him bad before he redeems him. There is a lot of anger in that depiction. Scrooge still colours our vision of 'greedy bankers'.

A *Christmas Carol* has shaped our view of what Christmas should be, but seldom is. If we ever catch ourselves feeling guilty as we survey the pile of presents under the tree or as we tuck into that seventh turkey sandwich, it is because of Charles Dickens. He brought guilt to the feast, because we are all too aware that few of us know how to 'keep Christmas' in the way that the reformed Scrooge did in later life.

Works of fiction are often described as 'capturing the public's imagination'. Very few really do. *A Christmas Carol* mostly definitely did. And still does.

Originally written for Norman Geras' normblog
in 2013 as Writer's choice 377

About Dickens

Charles Dickens was born on 7th February 1812 in Portsmouth, where his father was a clerk for the Royal Navy. He was the second of eight children. Dickens then lived in Bloomsbury in London and in Chatham in Kent before moving to Camden Town in London in 1822. His father was sent to the Marshalsea debtors' prison in Southwark in 1824, when Charles was 12, and Charles was sent to board with friends of the family.

Charles worked ten hours a day putting labels on pots of bootblacking in a factory near Charing Cross, before eventually being sent to Wellington House Academy in Camden. He then worked as a junior clerk in a law office, leaving to become a free-lance reporter in the law courts.

After a period as a journalist, Dickens became a hugely successful novelist, with work such as *Oliver Twist*, *Great Expectations*, *Nicholas Nickleby* and *David Copperfield*, most of which carried traces of his own life and childhood. He toured Britain and America giving readings and even planned to tour Australia. But he never forgot that troubled childhood.

Dickens was very concerned with the plight of poor children from the growing underclass of industrial Britain, and was passionately interested in their welfare and education, giving speeches and helping to raise funds for institutions like Great Ormond Street Hospital. Many of his books reflect this concern, not least *A Christmas Carol*, with the two feral children named as Ignorance and Want, who were the inspiration for my story.

Dickens wrote several Christmas stories, but *A Christmas Carol* was by far the most popular. He began work on it in 1843 and it was published in the same year, the first print run selling out on Christmas Eve.

Dickens was famous for his public readings and he read *A Christmas Carol* well over a hundred times. He read it at his last ever performance in 1870, the year he died.

Adaptations of A Christmas Carol

A *Christmas Carol* has never been out of print and has been adapted for the stage, film and television many times. There have been musical adaptations and animated versions, and its themes have been a clear influence on many other films and books, from *It's a Wonderful Life* and *The Grinch Who Stole Christmas* to *Groundhog Day*.

The many film adaptations of *A Christmas Carol* include a 1951 version with Alistair Simm brilliant as Scrooge, a 1970 musical version (called *Scrooge*) with Albert Finney in the lead role, *Scrooged* – a 1988 comedy update with Bill Murray in the lead – and *A Muppet Christmas Carol*, starring Michael Caine (and the Muppets of course). *Sesame Street* also had a go at its own version of *A Christmas Carol* in 2006. Patrick Stewart took the role of Scrooge in a television adaptation in 1999.

There have also been many animated versions of *A Christmas Carol* for television and cinema – most recently a 2009 computer animated 3D version by Disney with Jim Carrey voicing Scrooge (and the Spirits).

My own favourite is a Richard Williams animation from 1971, with Alistair Simm voicing Scrooge (as he had done in the earlier live-action movie). I remember watching it every Christmas morning (or so it seems now, looking back) throughout the Seventies. Shamefully, despite winning an Oscar for best animated short, it is not easily available as I write this.

A Christmas Carol is a story that each new generation seems to rediscover and reinvent, and there will doubtless be many more adaptations in the coming years.

READ ON FOR A TASTER OF
ANOTHER SPINE-TINGLING TALE
FROM THE MASTER OF THE MACABRE

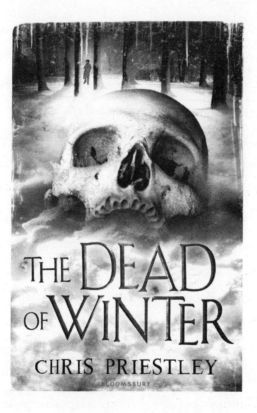

'Deliciously creepy with lots of twists and turns'
Daily Mail

PROLOGUE

My name is Michael: Michael Vyner. I'm going to tell you something of my life and of the strange events that have brought me to where I now sit, pen in hand, my heartbeat hastening at their recollection.

I hope that in the writing down of these things I will grow to understand my own story a little better and perhaps bring some comforting light to the still-dark, whispering recesses of my memory.

Horrors loom out of those shadows and my mind recoils at their approach. My God, I can still see that face – that terrible face. Those eyes! My hand clenches my pen with such strength I fear it will snap under the strain. It will take every ounce of willpower I possess to tell this tale. But tell it I must.

1

I had already known much hardship in my early years, but I had never before seen the horrible blackness of a soul purged of all that is good, shaped by resentment and hatred into something utterly vile and loveless. I had never known evil.

The story I am to recount may seem like the product of some fevered imagination, but the truth is the truth and all I can do is set it down as best I can, within the limits of my ability, and ask that you read it with an open mind.

If, after that, you turn away in disbelief, then I can do naught but smile and wish you well – and wish, too, that I could as easily free myself of the terrifying spectres that haunt the events I am about to relate.

So come with me now. We will walk back through time, and as the fog of the passing years rolls away we will find ourselves among the chill and weathered headstones of a large and well-stocked cemetery.

All about us are stone angels, granite obelisks and marble urns. A sleeping stone lion guards the grave of an old soldier, a praying angel that of a beloved child. Everywhere there are the inscriptions of remembrance, of love curdled into grief.

Grand tombs and mausoleums line a curving cobbled roadway, shaded beneath tall cypress trees. A hearse stands nearby, its black-plumed horses growing impatient. It is December and the air is as damp and cold as the graves beneath our feet. The morning mist is yet to clear. Fallen leaves still litter the cobbles.

A blackbird sings gaily, oblivious to the macabre surroundings, the sound ringing round the silent cemetery, sharp and sweet in the misty vagueness. Jackdaws fly overhead and seem to call back in answer. Some way off, a new grave coldly gapes and the tiny group of mourners are walking away, leaving a boy standing alone.

The boy has cried so much over the last few days that he thinks his tears must surely have dried up for ever. Yet, as he stares down at that awful wooden box in its frightful pit, the tears come again.

There are fewer things sadder than a poorly attended funeral. When that funeral is in honour of a dear and beloved mother, then that sadness is all the more sharply felt and bitter-tasting.

As I am certain by now you have guessed, the lonesome boy by that open grave is none other than the narrator of this story.

CHAPTER ONE

I looked into that grave with as much sense of dread and despair as if I had been staring into my own. Everything I loved was in that hateful wooden box below me. I was alone now: utterly alone.

I had never known my father. He was killed when I was but a baby, one of many whose lives were ended fighting for the British Empire in the bitter dust of Afghanistan. I had no extended family. My mother and I had been everything to each other.

But my mother had never been strong, though she had borne her hardships with great courage. She endured her illness with the same fortitude. But courage is not always enough.

These thoughts and many others taunted me beside that grave. I half considered leaping in and joining her. It seemed preferable to the dark and thorny path that lay ahead of me.

As I stood poised at the pit's edge, I heard footsteps behind me and turned to see my mother's lawyer, Mr Bentley, walking towards me accompanied by a tall, smart and expensively-dressed man. I had, of course, noticed him during the funeral and wondered who he might be. His face was long and pale, his nose large but sharply sculpted. It was a face made for the serious and mournful expression it now wore.

'Michael,' said Bentley, 'this is Mr Jerwood.'

'Master Vyner,' said the man, touching the brim of his hat. 'If I might have a quiet word.'

Bentley left us alone, endeavouring to walk backwards and stumbling over a tombstone as he rejoined his wife, who had been standing at a respectful distance. Looking at Jerwood again, I thought I recognised him.

'I'm sorry, sir,' I said, gulping back sobs and hastily brushing the tears from my cheeks. 'But do I know you?'

'We have met, Michael,' he replied, 'but you will undoubtedly have been too young to remember. May I call you Michael?' I made no reply and he smiled a half-smile, taking my silence for assent.

'Excellent. In short, Michael, you do not know me, but I know you very well.'

'Are you a friend of my mother's, sir?' I asked, puzzled at who this stranger could possibly be.

'Alas no,' he said, glancing quickly towards the grave and then back to me. 'Though I did meet your mother on several occasions, I could not say we were friends. In fact, I could not say with all honesty that your mother actually liked me. Rather, I should have to confess – if I were pressed by a judge in a court of law – that your mother actively *dis*liked me. Not that I ever let that in any way influence me in my dealings with her, and I would happily state – before the same hypothetical judge – that I held your late mother in the highest esteem.'

The stranger breathed a long sigh at the end of this speech, as if the effort of it had quite exhausted him.

'But I'm sorry, sir,' I said. 'I still do not understand . . .'

'You do not understand who I am,' he said with a smile, shaking his head. 'What a fool. Forgive me.' He removed the glove from his right hand and extended it towards me with a small bow. 'Tristan Jerwood,' he said, 'of Enderby, Pettigrew and

Jerwood. I represent the interests of Sir Stephen Clarendon.'

I made no reply. I had heard this name before, of course. It was Sir Stephen whom my father had died to save in an act of bravery that drew great praise and even made the newspapers.

But I had never been able to take pride in his sacrifice. I felt angry that my father had thrown his life away to preserve that of a man I did not know. This hostility clearly showed in my face. Mr Jerwood's expression became cooler by several degrees.

'You have heard that name, I suspect?' he asked.

'I have, sir,' I replied. 'I know that he helped us after my father died. With money and so forth. I had thought that Sir Stephen might be here himself.'

Jerwood heard – as I had wanted him to hear – the note of reproach in my voice and pursed his lips, sighing a little and looking once again towards the grave.

'Your mother did not like me, Michael, as I have said,' he explained, without looking back. 'She took Sir Stephen's money and help because she had to, for her sake and for yours, but she only ever took the barest minimum of what was offered. She was a very proud woman, Michael. I always respected

8

that. Your mother resented the money – and her need for it – and resented me for being the intermediary. That is why she insisted on employing her own lawyer.'

Here he glanced across at Mr Bentley, who stood waiting for me by the carriage with his wife. I had been staying with the Bentleys in the days leading up to the funeral. I had met him on many occasions before, though only briefly, but they had been kind and generous. My pain was still so raw, however, that even such a tender touch served only to aggravate it.

'She was a fine woman, Michael, and you are a very lucky lad to have had her as a mother.'

Tears sprang instantly to my eyes.

'I do not feel so very lucky now, sir,' I said.

Jerwood put his hand on my shoulder. 'Now, now,' he said quietly. 'Sir Stephen has been through troubled times himself. I do not think this is the right time to speak of them, but I promise you that had they not been of such an extreme nature, he would have been at your side today.'

A tear rolled down my cheek. I shrugged his hand away.

'I thank you for coming, sir – for coming in his place,' I said coolly. I was in no mood to be comforted by some stranger whom, by his own admission, my mother did not like.

Jerwood gave his gloves a little twist as though he were wringing the neck of an imaginary chicken. Then he sighed and gave his own neck a stretch.

'Michael,' he said, 'it is my duty to inform you of some matters concerning your immediate future.'

I had naturally given this much thought myself, with increasingly depressing results. Who was I now? I was some non-person, detached from all family ties, floating free and friendless.

'Sir Stephen is now your legal guardian,' he said.

'But I thought my mother did not care for Sir Stephen or for you,' I said, taken aback a little. 'Why would she have agreed to such a thing?'

'I need not remind you that you have no one else, Michael,' said Jerwood. 'But let me assure you that your mother was in full agreement. She loved you and she knew that whatever her feelings about the matter, this was the best option.'

I looked away. He was right, of course. What choice did I have?

'You are to move schools,' said Jerwood.

'Move schools?' I said. 'Why?'

'Sir Stephen feels that St Barnabas is not quite suitable for the son – the ward, I should say – of a man such as him.'

'But I am happy where I am,' I said stiffly.

Jerwood's mouth rose almost imperceptibly at the corners.

'That is not what I have read in the letters Sir Stephen has received from the headmaster.'

I blushed a little from both embarrassment and anger at this stranger knowing about my personal affairs.

'This could be a new start for you, Michael.'

'I do not want a new start, sir,' I replied.

Jerwood let out a long breath, which rose as mist in front of his face. He turned and looked away.

'Do not fight this,' said Jerwood, as if to the trees. 'Sir Stephen has your best interests at heart, believe me. In any event, he can tell you so himself.' He turned back to face me. 'You are invited to visit him for Christmas. He is expecting you at Hawton Mere tomorrow evening.'

'Tomorrow evening?' I cried in astonishment.

'Yes,' said Jerwood. 'I shall accompany you myself. We shall catch a train from –'

'I won't go!' I snapped.

Jerwood took a deep breath and nodded at

Bentley, who hurried over, rubbing his hands together and looking anxiously from my face to Jerwood's.

'Is everything settled then?' he asked, his nose having ripened to a tomato red in the meantime. 'All is well?'

Bentley was a small and rather stout gentleman who seemed unwilling to accept how stout he was. His clothes were at least one size too small for him and gave him a rather alarming appearance, as if his buttons might fly off at any moment or he himself explode with a loud pop.

This impression of over-inflation, of over-ripeness, was only exacerbated by his perpetually red and perspiring face. And if all that were not enough, Bentley was prone to the most unnerving twitches – twitches that could vary in intensity from a mere tic or spasm to startling convulsions.

'I have informed Master Vyner of the situation regarding his schooling,' said Jerwood, backing away from Bentley a little. He tipped his hat to each of us. 'I have also informed him of his visit to Sir Stephen. I shall bid you farewell. Until tomorrow, gentlemen.'

I felt a wave of misery wash over me as I stood there with the twitching Bentley. A child's fate is always in the hands of others; a child is always so very powerless. But how I envied those children whose fates were held in the loving grip of their parents and not, like mine, guided by the cold and joyless hands of lawyers.

'But see now,' said Bentley, twitching violently. 'There now. Dear me. All will be well. All will be well, you'll see.'

'But I don't want to go,' I said. 'Please, Mr Bentley, could I not spend Christmas with you?'

Bentley twitched and winced.

'Now see here, Michael,' he said. 'This is very hard. Very hard indeed.'

'Sir?' I said, a little concerned at his distress and what might be causing it.

'I'm afraid that much as Mrs Bentley and I would love to have you come and stay with us, we both feel that it is only right that you should accept Sir Stephen's invitation.'

'I see,' I said. I was embarrassed to find myself on the verge of tears again and I looked away so that Bentley might not see my troubled face.

'Now then,' he said, grabbing my arms with both hands and turning me back to face him. 'He is your guardian, Michael. You are the ward of a very wealthy man and your whole life depends upon him. Would you throw that away for one Christmas?'

'Would he?' I asked. 'Would he disown me because I stay with you and not him?'

'I would hope not,' he said. 'But you never know with the rich. I work with them all the time and, let me tell you, they are a rum lot. And if the rich are strange, then the landed gentry are stranger still. You never know what any of them will do . . .'

Bentley came to a halt here, realising he had strayed from the point.

'Go to Hawton Mere for Christmas,' he said quietly. 'That's my advice. That's free advice from a lawyer, Michael. It is as rare and as lovely as a phoenix.'

'No,' I said, refusing to change my grim mood. 'I will not.'

Bentley looked at the ground, rocked back and forth on his heels once or twice, then exhaled noisily.

'I have something for you, my boy. Your dear mother asked me to give this to you when the time came.'

With those words he pulled an envelope from his inside coat pocket and handed it to me. Without asking what it was, I opened it and read the enclosed letter.

Dear Michael,

You know that I have always hated taking anything from that man whose life your dear father saved so nobly at the expense of his own. But though each time I did receive his help it made me all the more aware of my husband's absence and it pained my heart – still I took it, Michael, because of you.

And now, because of you, I write this letter while I still have strength, because I know how proud you are. Michael, it is my wish – my dying wish – that you graciously accept all that Sir Stephen can offer you. Take his money and his opportunities and make something of yourself. Be everything you can. Do this for me, Michael.

As always and for ever,
Your loving mother

I folded the letter up and Bentley handed me a handkerchief for the tears that now filled my eyes. What argument could I have that could triumph against such a letter? It seemed I had no choice.

Bentley put his arm round me. 'There, there,' he said. 'All will be well, all will be well. Hawton Mere has a moat, they tell me. A moat! You shall be like a knight in a castle, eh? A knight!' And at this, he waved his finger about in flamboyant imitation of a sword. 'A moated manor house, eh? Yes, yes. All will be well.'

I dried my tears and exhaustion came over me. Resistance was futile and I had no energy left to pursue my objection.

'Come, my boy,' said Bentley quietly. 'Let us quit this place. The air of the graveyard is full of evil humours – toxic, you know, very toxic indeed. Why, I knew a man who dropped down dead as he walked away from a funeral – dead before he reached his carriage. Quite, quite dead.'

Bentley ushered me towards his carriage and we climbed inside. The carriage creaked forward, the wheels beginning their rumble. I looked out of the window and saw my mother's grave retreat from view, lost among the numberless throng of tombs and headstones.

LOOK OUT FOR MORE FROM THE MASTER OF THE MACABRE

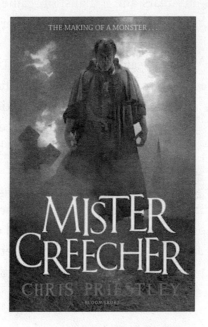

'A brilliant counterpoint to
Frankenstein, compellingly written'
Chris Riddell

'This exciting, affecting and bloody story is a
clever tribute to an enduring classic'
Financial Times

'A beautifully written gothic metafiction'
The Times

LOOK OUT FOR MORE FROM
THE MASTER OF THE MACABRE

'*Through Dead Eyes* is unbearably gripping'
The Times

'A creepy, tightly plotted psychological thriller . . . chilling'
Telegraph

LOOK OUT FOR

THE
TALES OF TERROR
COLLECTION

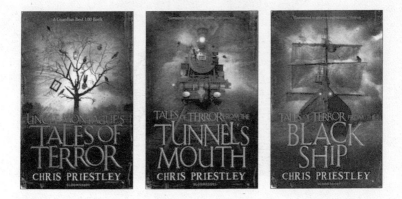

'Wonderfully macabre and beautifully
crafted horror stories'
Chris Riddell

'Guaranteed to give you nightmares'
Observer

'A delightfully scary book'
Irish Times